# Smith's
## MONTHLY

*Every Month Original
Novels, Stories, and Articles*

*USA Today Bestselling Writer*
**Dean Wesley Smith**

# TABLE OF CONTENTS

# Smith's Monthly Issue #23

All Contents copyright © 2015 Dean Wesley Smith
Published by WMG Publishing
Cover and interior design copyright © 2015 WMG Publishing
Cover art copyright © by Andrew7726/Dreamstime.com

"Introduction: A Very Short Novel" copyright © 2015 Dean Wesley Smith

"Fighting the Fuzzy Wuzzy" copyright © 2015 Dean Wesley Smith, cover design copyright © 2015 WMG Publishing, cover art by Cthoman/Dreamstime.com and Dole/Dreamstime.com

"Husband Dummies" copyright © 2015 Dean Wesley Smith, cover design copyright © 2015 WMG Publishing.

"A Golden Dream" copyright © 2015 Dean Wesley Smith, cover design copyright © 2015 WMG Publishing.

*An Easy Shot* copyright © 2015 Dean Wesley Smith, cover design copyright © 2015 WMG Publishing, cover art by Fotoslaz/Dreamstime.com

"Last Car for this Time" copyright © 2015 Dean Wesley Smith, cover design copyright © 2015 WMG Publishing

"On Top of the Dead" copyright © 2015 Dean Wesley Smith, cover design copyright © 2015 WMG Publishing

"The Yellow of the Flickering Past" copyright © 2015 Dean Wesley Smith, cover design copyright © 2015 WMG Publishing

*Heaven Painted as a Cop Car* copyright © 2015 Dean Wesley Smith, cover design copyright © 2015 WMG Publishing, cover art by Andrew7726 /Dreamstime.com

The Writings and Opinions of

# Dean Wesley Smith

## Introduction
## A VERY SHORT NOVEL

I will often talk to students and in my blog about writing the story to the length the story wants to be written. And not one word more.

This month's issue contains an example of that practice with the cover short novel, or novella as many people call them.

Back when I was writing for New York publishers, a book had to be a contracted length, usually between 80,000 and 100,000 words.

Each contract would vary and I wrote a few novels for the traditional publishers around 70,000, but almost all of them clocked in around 80,000 words or more.

But the problem with that demand, actually written into a contract, was the story sometimes just didn't have enough in it to be an 80,000 word story.

So what happened?

Padding, that's what happened.

I would have to go back into the book and figure out where the characters could take a side trip, roam off chasing something or make up something that could be solved in the needed amount of words so the story could move forward again.

Think of it this way. A story line is like a freeway. You drive on the freeway from point one to the exit point. But if that freeway of that story is only 50,000 words and a contract demands 80,000 words, then the characters needed to take an off ramp along the way and roam out in the countryside for some made-up reason before coming back on the freeway to continue to the end of the trip.

Filler.

Padding.

Whatever you wanted to call it.

And I hated that.

I grew up reading in the 1950s and 1960s, when the average length of a novel was 30,000 words. Novels ranged from

---

# Thanks for the Support

## Dean Wesley Smith

25,000 to 45,000 words for the really long ones. I loved books of that length and still do. They were what I grew up reading.

So doing all the padding for over a hundred novels in traditional publishing always bothered me and I didn't much like it. I felt that it hurt some stories, actually.

So when publishing changed six or seven years ago, I swore I would never write another padded novel, no matter what. I would write the stories at the length the story wanted to be.

Not one word more.

So how did the short novel or novella in this issue come about?

As many of you know, in July of 2015 I wrote a story per day. And I had a blast doing so. Three of those stories were clearly part of a novel in my Ghost of a Chance series. The stories stood alone as short stories just fine. But together they built a larger picture.

So I had those clearly in my head and wanted to write the rest of the story that went along with the three stories.

So I went through them, blending them into the novel, having fun. And then suddenly the story was finished. There will be other stories with the two characters down the road, but the longer novel I wanted to write about the two characters meeting was finished.

But it was only around 20,000 words.

And for a short moment I was tempted to try to expand it.

Then I remembered how much I hated doing that and decided to just leave it alone.

So in this volume the anchor novel is a very short novel.

And you get more short stories to fill out the magazine.

As I have said before here: I love this new world. I have the freedom to just stop when the story is finished.

I hope you enjoy the results.

*—Dean Wesley Smith*
*August 18, 2015*
*Lincoln City, Oregon*

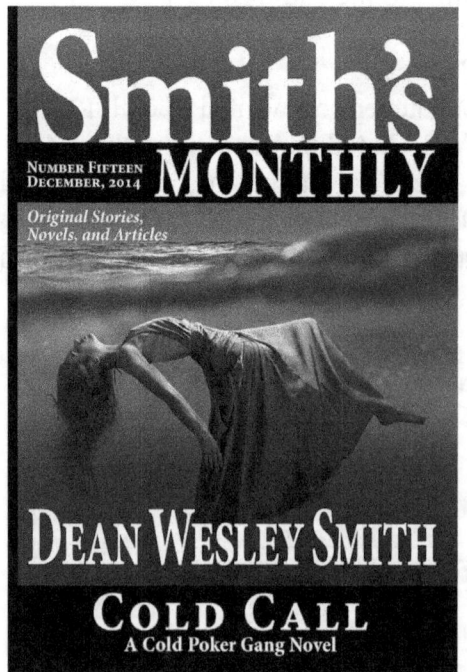

# Coming Next Issue in Smith's Monthly
# BAD BEAT
## A New Cold Poker Gang Mystery

*The world about to be destroyed. What can a poker player do?*

*When a blue Searchlight appears and says the world hangs on the edge of destruction, even a great poker face feels hard to keep. Until Poker Boy discovers the blue guy doesn't bluff.*

*Can a simple superhero save the world?*

*Sometimes playing poker might be the answer for just about everything.*

# FIGHTING THE FUZZY-WUZZY
## *A Poker Boy Story*

## ONE

**I FIRST MET** Wolfgang Sucker two nights before the great Fuzzy-Wuzzy war.

Now, as Poker Boy, I meet my share of strange beings, mostly just people sitting around poker tables as I try to earn enough to get to the next place where I have to do my superhero thing and rescue someone or fight the bad guy. (And sometimes along the way I even save a dog or two, but that's not part of my job description. It just sort of happens.)

But Wolfgang Sucker was one of the stranger people who ever walked up to me and asked for help.

Honestly, I didn't see him until he was standing in front of me. I was standing against one of the large stone columns in the main lobby of the MGM Grand Hotel and Casino on the Strip in Las Vegas. My girlfriend and sidekick, Patty Ledgerwood, aka Front Desk Girl, had a couple of things to finish before she got off work and we headed back to her place.

I have no idea how Wolfgang Sucker knew who I was, and I sure didn't notice him until he was standing in front of me.

"Poker Boy?" he asked, his voice sounding like someone sanding a piece of furniture. "I need your help if you don't mind. My name is Wolfgang Sucker."

Actually, what he really needed was a couple bottles of Scope and a bath. His breath smelled like he had bathed in onions, but I didn't say anything. Not my place to judge people who are asking for my help.

That was the exact moment, as the crowds of people moved around and past us in the huge lobby, talking and laughing, that I actually focused on Wolfgang Sucker for the first time.

And actually saw him, in all of his blueness.

Not kidding. He was blue, skin and all, and there was a lot of skin showing. He only wore a pair of tight pants that seemed more like skin than pants, showing parts that no man should show in public without getting arrested.

If the blue had been painted on I would have thought him to be a refugee from the Blue Man Group that performed all the time in Vegas. But his skin was a real blue.

He had on no shirt at all, but security in the MGM Grand didn't seem to even notice. In fact no one seemed to notice.

He stood about six inches taller than my six-foot frame and weighed far under my weight, which gave Wolfgang the look of a tall stick with arms. I had seen skinnier people, but not many. Skinnier people were usually high school basketball players, and Wolfgang looked to be a ways from high school age, even though his skin was as blue and smooth as it comes.

Besides being blue, what made Wolfgang really stand out was his nervous tick of constantly turning his head from side to side, not fast, but slowly, like a lighthouse beacon moving around.

He seldom looked at anyone directly with his deep blue eyes. His gaze just sort of passed over you until his head was completely sideways to you, then it slowly came back the other direction.

After about two minutes of talking with him that first time, I wanted to just grab his head and hold it still, but I was afraid his body would start rotating under it. And I didn't want to get that close to that breath, either.

But worse yet, if that and the bad breath wasn't bad enough, his head was completely bald and covered in white tattoo patterns of some weird alien design that looked at first a little like a giant net with a squid in the middle. But every time he turned his head and then started back, the tattoos seemed to shift without really shifting so that by the time his head was turned one hundred and eighty degrees in the other direction, the scars gave a different image.

And they moved around, all over his face, his head, down his neck.

Never once did the image repeat that I could tell.

I have no idea how the tattoos changed, but I sure watched them a lot trying to figure it out since there was no point trying to look the guy in the eyes. At one point I actually thought about fighting my way upstream into the onions to get closer to see how those marks were shifting like that. But I didn't.

After a moment or two of staring at Wolfgang Sucker's head, I realized he had been talking about something, but his rasping voice was so low I couldn't hear it over the loud sounds of the huge lobby and the casino down the hallway.

I held up my hand for him to stop. "We're going to need to get to a place where we can talk in a little more quiet. I'm having trouble hearing you. Can you hold on for less than one minute?"

I could see Patty heading toward us across the lobby, and I most certainly wanted her to hear what kind of help this guy needed from me. And I wanted her to meet him, otherwise she would just never believe me.

As she approached, Wolfgang Sucker turned and bowed just slightly at the waist. "Front Desk Girl. Good, I was also hoping you might help as well."

Patty's eyes got round and she glanced at me before going back to staring at Wolfgang Sucker as he introduced himself.

I just shrugged and indicated I didn't know what the guy wanted.

It was a nice, comfortable October night outside, so I figured there would be less noise out through the front doors than in the lobby, so I indicated we should all move that way.

He wouldn't budge. "No," he said firmly. "The Fuzzy-Wuzzys are going to be arriving out there, near the front door."

Now Patty's eyes really got large, and I'm sure I had the worst puzzled look on my face. It was then that it occurred to me that this might be some practical joke, played on us by one of the gambling gods.

In fact, the more I thought about, the more I was sure it was a joke. The only "Fuzzy-Wuzzy" I knew came from an old children's rhyme about a bald bear or something like that.

I slipped Patty and me out of time, leaving old Wolfgang frozen with the rest of the lobby.

I always got a kick out of doing that. It was a real power, compared to some of my other powers like getting someone to believe me or reading their faces to see if they were telling the truth. Slipping into a moment in time was just fun and cool. I couldn't hold it very long, not more than a few minutes, but each time I did it, I got stronger. And since all my power came from casinos, it was pretty easy to do while standing inside one of the bigger ones on the planet.

"Is this guy for real?" Patty asked, staring at the scars on his head that were

now frozen in the moment into a picture of some sort of alien cow being eaten by some other creature with fangs.

"I have no idea," I said. "I'm guessing it's a joke someone's pulling on us. It finally dawned on me that with a name like Wolfgang Sucker, we might be the real suckers. And it was the Fuzzy-Wuzzy part that convinced me."

Patty nodded, so I shouted into the air, "Stan!"

An instant later Stan appeared beside us. It only took him a second to notice Wolfgang and start staring, his mouth open.

"So what's the joke?" I asked.

Stan didn't answer, just sort of walked around Wolfgang, then came back to me.

"No joke," Stan said. "This guy is a Searchlight. I've only seen one and that was a number of centuries back."

"Searchlight?" Patty asked.

"Yeah, the name we call them, more than likely because of that annoying head movement they do. There are only a few thousand of them and they live forever, or so the myths say. No one knows where they came from, where they live, or what they even do. Or what those changing pictures on their heads mean."

"You're serious?" I asked, still thinking this was an elaborate joke that Stan was part of.

"Completely," Stan said, still staring at Wolfgang. "Did he say what he wanted?"

"My help is all I managed to hear because he talks so softly."

Stan frowned. "Not good, really not good."

"And he wanted me to help as well," Patty said. "And he knew who I was."

Okay, maybe this wasn't a joke. I sure didn't like the sound of the God of Poker saying "Not good, really not good." In all the years I had worked as a superhero for him, he had never said anything like that. Even joking.

"He wouldn't go outside to talk because he said the Fuzzy-Wuzzys were going to be out there, or something like that."

"Oh, shit," Stan said, his normally calm face now almost pale.

Having the God of Poker looked scared about a guy named after a hairless bear didn't make me feel any better about this situation either. I had no idea what the problem even was and I was starting to panic.

Stan turned to Patty. "Get our guest to a meeting room. I'll be back with Laverne and some other help as soon as I can. And you had better call in your team."

At that Stan vanished.

"Seems our nice evening at your place has just been postponed," I said.

All Patty could do was nod as I stuck us back into real time and let the noise of the crowd wash back over us like a pounding wave. Being in the silence of between-time was always nice.

Patty indicated that Wolfgang Sucker should follow her. "I have a meeting room we can talk in."

"Have you contacted Laverne and the others?" Wolfgang asked in his raspy voice, barely loud enough for me to hear.

"We have," I said. "They'll join us in the meeting room."

He said simply, "Good. We will need everyone if we are to survive this coming battle."

I stared at him as we walked, not liking the sound of that either. And if he wanted to contact Laverne, why didn't he just go to her?

And then he said, just loud enough for me to hear, "And we are called

Searchlights because we stand guard over humanity, always watching for trouble, not because of our head movement."

I walked a few steps with my mouth open. Even with Patty and me out of time, he had overheard what we had said.

That was creepy, just creepy.

# TWO

**THE MEETING ROOM** that Patty led us to was off the main corridor leading to the casino from the lobby, and it could hold fifty people, if needed. It was the standard business meeting room that you saw everywhere in every hotel. Only this one had the bright MGM Grand Hotel colors and logo on the carpet and a huge polished wooden table in the middle of the room with about thirty leather chairs around it.

When Patty closed the door, the sounds from outside shut off as if someone had thrown a switch. I had no doubt that in this place I would be able to actually hear Wolfgang speak clearly in his rasping voice, but he didn't say anything and I had no idea what to ask him.

I was still trying to get over the fact that he could hear us between moments in time.

He moved with gliding steps to the head of the table and stood behind the leather chair there and said nothing. His head just kept shifting from side to side, slowly.

Patty jumped on her cell phone and called both Screamer and The Smoke and told them where we were.

"They are both about ten minutes away," Patty said.

"Good," I said. I didn't say that I wished I knew what we were up against so I could tell them what was going on.

A moment later Stan, the God of Poker, appeared with Burt, the God of Casino Operations, and Laverne, Lady Luck herself. Laverne was dressed in a black pants suit.

Now I knew for sure this was no joke.

Stan and Burt just looked worried.

"Wolfgang," she said, moving toward our guest. "It is always a pleasure to see you again.

Then Lady Luck bowed slightly in a show of respect, which flat stunned me. Laverne was one of the most powerful gods there was in all the deities. She didn't bow to anyone I knew of.

At least until now.

Wolfgang bowed slightly in the same way to Laverne as he had done to Patty. "It is also good to see you," he said, his voice clear even though it sounded more like someone was taking sandpaper to the large wooden meeting table in the room.

Laverne got right to the point. "Am I to understand that the Fuzzy-Wuzzys are coming back?"

"They are," Wolfgang said, his head never stopping for an instant.

"How long until they reach this plane of existence?" Laverne asked.

"They will become clear to you in five hours, and to the rest of the human race in two days; just under forty-nine of your hours. If they cannot be stopped before that point, I fear for the human race."

I glanced at my watch. It was just past eleven in the evening. So they would appear to humans in two days at midnight. Whatever they were. And Laverne would be able to see them coming in five hours.

And I assumed something called a Fuzzy-Wuzzy appearing suddenly to humans was a bad thing from the way everyone was acting and talking. But at this point I didn't have a clue why or how we were all going to die.

And I also didn't know where they were appearing from exactly. Laverne and Wolfgang sure seemed to think all this was serious. For the moment, since Laverne was the big boss, that was good enough for me.

"Are there other Searchlights involved?" Laverne asked.

"We all are," Wolfgang Sucker said. "At the moment they are contacting all the other deities, and a delegation has been sent to the Fates. We have little time."

Now I really wanted to know why this guy came to me first.

Laverne nodded. "I assume this is a worldwide attack this time?"

"It is," Wolfgang said. "They are stronger and are coming in more numbers than before. They will not be easily tricked or defeated this time."

"Humanity barely survived the last time," Laverne said, shaking her head.

Now that didn't sound good at all.

Patty took my hand and squeezed it.

"And why are you here?" Laverne asked. "Is this an attack point?"

"Yes, they are opening a portal just in front of this building. One of a thousand such portals around the world."

"A thousand?" Laverne asked softly, more to herself than to Wolfgang.

He said nothing.

Laverne again bowed slightly to Wolfgang Sucker. "Thank you and your people for the warning and the help in this coming fight. As always, it is appreciated."

"Unless I am needed before, I will come back to this room in twelve hours," he said, returning the bow.

Then he vanished.

"Damn," Laverne said, turning to the rest of us shaking her head. "I worried about this day coming again. I just hoped it never would."

Now the silence in the large meeting room felt like a huge weight just pressing down on everything.

"Stan," Laverne said, "please explain to Poker Boy and his team what's happening."

Then she and Burt vanished.

Stan moved over to the table and sat down hard.

Seeing the God of Poker completely shaken and hearing Lady Luck herself actually swear wasn't a good sign.

Not good at all.


# THREE


**PATTY AND I** went around the big table and sat facing Stan. Patty kept her hand in mine and I liked that. Together we were a lot stronger than we were apart. And from the sounds of whatever we were fighting, we were going to need all the strength we could muster.

I wanted to ask Stan about a thousand questions starting off with why something that could destroy mankind was called a "Fuzzy-Wuzzy" and why, if this Searchlight guy wanted to talk to Laverne, did he come to me first, but I decided to just wait. It sounded like these blue guys were a lot older than some silly children's rhyme and more than likely had some ritual they had to follow.

Both Screamer and The Smoke came through the door two minutes later, for a moment letting in the loud sounds from the hallway and casino before closing the door.

Screamer was a superhero as well and his main power was the ability to connect minds of people and put images in people's heads. He got his name from a time when the police asked him to get the location of a buried-alive woman from a killer's mind. He made the guy scream and the nickname stuck.

The Smoke is a superhero working for the animal deities. He's actually a werewolf of sorts, with complete control of which form he is in, and he can go through walls with ease. That's a nifty trick that has come in handy a few times since he became part of our team.

"So what are we in for this time?" Screamer asked dropping into one of the soft leather chairs and smiling.

Then he noticed that Patty and I and Stan were all looking very upset.

"I fear this is no good," The Smoke said, moving around and standing off to my right near the wall. The Smoke liked to stand, and only sat when he needed to.

Stan nodded and took a deep breath. "It's bad and everyone is working on this. The Fuzzy-Wuzzys are coming back."

"Oh, no," The Smoke said, coming over and also dropping into a chair beside me.

It seemed clear that he knew what the Fuzzy-Wuzzys were. Screamer just looked as puzzled as I felt.

"Okay," I said to Stan. "Time to tell us what these things are."

"History first. Do you know the story of the continent of Atlantis?"

"Was that a real place?" Patty asked a fraction of a moment before I did.

"It was the home of most humans on the planet at the time," Stan said. "A wonderful place, very beautiful. It was mankind's third home on this planet, and it was destroyed in the first Fuzzy-Wuzzy invasion."

I desperately wanted to ask him what the first two homes were and where they were and how old was he, but I managed to stay on topic somehow. At this point I had so many questions there was no chance I was going to remember them all.

"How did they destroy Atlantis?" Patty asked.

"They didn't, we did," Stan said. "We sank it to kill them and drive them back."

I could hear a pin drop in that huge meeting room at that moment. Stan seemed very far away and didn't want to meet my gaze at all.

"You sank it?"

He nodded. "All the gods combined, along with the Fates and help from the Searchlights. We all sank it. We killed almost a billion humans to save everyone else. Humanity almost didn't recover."

Again the silence filled the room, and my stomach felt like it was going to crawl up through my throat and lodge in my nose. I just couldn't think of one damn thing to say.

Patty squeezed my hand really, really hard.

"Why are these Fuzzy-Wuzzy things so bad?" Screamer finally asked.

"Humans are a giant buffet to them," Stan said. "They eat everything except bones and fingernails and hair."

"They also eat most animals," The Smoke said. "And trees and brush and everything."

"Where do they come from?" Patty asked.

"They are coming from the alternation dimension over down the time stream," Stan said.

I felt like a kid in school and the teacher was talking, but nothing was making sense. "Do you want to try to explain that?" I asked, "or for now can we just say they come from another dimension?"

Stan nodded. "Just say another parallel dimension, only the humans in all the dimensions in that direction along the time stream lost the war to the Fuzzy-Wuzzys and are gone. We are their next meal. But we managed to stop them so soundly last time that it has taken them thousands of years to recover."

Again the silence.

"So what do these things look like?" I asked. "Why the name Fuzzy-Wuzzy? And why can't we get the armies of the world to pitch into this fight?"

Stan pointed to the nail on his little finger. "They are bugs, covered in a light fur, and over a hundred of them could fit on my little fingernail."

I just stared at him. "You are telling me this great threat to humanity is a mass invasion of tiny, tiny, furry bed bugs?"

He nodded. "They can take a human body down to a pile of bones and Fuzzy-Wuzzy black shit in two seconds. And once here they can move faster than any man can run. In Atlantis I watched them mow through a crowd of thousands before the crowd knew what hit it. The more they eat and digest, the smarter they get and the harder they are to stop."

I opened my mouth and again could think of nothing to say.

"So you drowned them the last time?" Screamer finally asked.

Stan nodded. "We did, and poured an awful lot of ocean water through the dimensional portals. But they only came through five portals last time, not like the thousands they are attacking through this time."

It finally dawned on me what was bothering me.

"You are telling me these things are very, very tiny. Yet you are acting like they are intelligent. That's not possible."

"Hive mind," Stan said. "Alone or in groups of only a few thousand, they have no ability to think and can be easily killed. In fact, in groups of under a thousand they don't eat. But in masses, they are eating and thinking machines of fantastic ability and intellect. Somehow they transport the energy from eating to the hive mind. No one is sure how that works."

"So what weapons kill them?" Screamer asked. "And can anything protect a human from them?"

"Stepping on them kills them," Stan said. "Drowning, flame, anything with any force. And chemicals of all types kill them. Just like any other tiny bugs. The problem is that they move so fast and together that they can lose millions and not be bothered in the slightest."

"And protection?"

"They can't eat through anything inorganic," Stan said. "Stone, rock, rubber, things like that. But they can go through wood like it doesn't exist."

Again the intense silence.

I couldn't think of another question to ask Stan, and neither could anyone else it seemed, so Stan nodded and said, "I'll be back in an hour to see if you four have any ideas on how to fight these things."

Then he vanished.

The silence again. I was starting to really, really hate the silence.

Finally I said, "We are so screwed."

None of my team challenged me on that.

# FOUR

After we all sat there in the silence for what seemed like the longest time, I finally couldn't take it anymore. "Anyone up for a milkshake?"

Normally we met downtown, at The Diner, to plan operations and work to save people. It just seemed natural to go there now. It wasn't more than a small hole-in-the-wall around the corner on a side street from the Horseshoe Casino. The Diner was decorated in fake 1960s stuff and had a phony jukebox playing in the background all the time.

Before anyone could say anything, Stan showed back up. "I would love a milkshake."

A moment later we all appeared in The Diner sitting at our favorite booth while Stan sat in a chair in front of the booth. Madge, our normal waitress, was sitting at the counter shaking her head. In all the years we had been coming into this little place, I had never seen Madge sit down. She was a superhero working for the Gods of Food and Beverage, and she knew about us.

Madge always had an attitude, and was the best waitress I had ever met. And when in the 1960s diner uniform, she always wore too much make-up and light slacks three sizes too tight. She was a large woman both top and bottom, and it was a standing joke that no one should be allowed to watch Madge walk away or bend over.

Since we discovered she was a superhero as well, she had become a sort of unofficial member of my team.

We were the only ones in The Diner, and it was clear the place was closed, something I had also never seen. At least the oldies station was still playing softly on the radio.

Stan shouted over to Madge. "Our regular, then come join us. We've got planning to do."

Madge glanced around and it was clear from the black streaks of thick make-up on her face that she had been crying. She must have heard about humanity's upcoming doom.

She nodded and got to her feet, using a napkin to smear the make-up even more.

"So when are you going to teach me that jumping around in space trick?" I asked Stan. I'd been bugging him about learning that now for a while, but he had just never gotten around to showing me how that power worked. He had never said I didn't have the power, only that I needed to learn how to do it.

"Next week," he said, 'if we can figure out a way to win this war, and there is a next week."

I nodded. "Deal. Now tell me why the Searchlight came to me instead of going straight to Laverne?"

"Custom," Stan said. "When you want to see the queen, you don't just barge into the throne room, you talk to her guards."

"Real old school," I said.

Stan just nodded.

From the counter the milkshake machines started up.

"So how come you are back here with us?" Patty asked.

"I'm worthless with the gods," he said. "I told Laverne I'd do better back here with your team, and she agreed."

Over the years, our team had saved the planet a couple of times, and saved Lady Luck herself more than once. She clearly had a lot of faith in us to send Stan to help us. I just wished I had as much faith in us right now as Lady Luck did.

I was just a lowly poker-playing superhero. What could I do against an invasion of tiny bugs? I couldn't read their faces because more than likely they didn't have any. I couldn't take their money, or bluff them off their chips. And I...

"Bluff," I said out loud.

Everyone at the table looked at me.

I had zero idea what I meant by that, but my little voice, the voice that told me when to bet and when to fold, was shouting that the key to all this was bluffing. And I trusted that little voice.

But how the hell do you bluff a hive mind of millions of bugs?

"You want to explain that outburst?" Stan said.

I glanced around the booth, realizing that everyone was just staring at me. Madge was just finishing the milkshakes.

"Not sure what I meant," I said. "I need more information. Wolfgang said that they are coming through one thousand portals? How big is a portal?"

"In Atlantis a portal was about five feet around, but impossible to block."

"And we know where all these portals are going to appear?" I asked.

Stan nodded. "The Searchlights do, and the top gods will be able to see them forming in a few more hours as well."

I wish I could figure out what I was thinking. It was just there, at the back of my mind, but darned if I could figure it out.

Then I had another idea.

I took Patty's hand that had been resting on my right leg and placed it on the top of the table with my hand on top of hers. Then I looked at Screamer.

"I have an idea, but can't quite get it to form. Come on in with Patty and help me figure it out."

Screamer nodded, reached across the table, and put his hand on top of ours.

Suddenly Screamer and Patty were in my mind. We had joined minds so many times on missions over the last few years, the sensation almost felt familiar.

Weird, but familiar.

Bluff. What am I thinking about, bluffing the Fuzzy-Wuzzy?

I focused, trying to dig up the idea as Screamer and Patty searched inside my head. After what seemed like only an instant Screamer thought at me directly, Just what the word means. To mislead.

He's right, Patty thought at me. You are thinking we can mislead the Fuzzy-Wuzzy.

Screamer took his hand away and I was again alone in my own head. But I did have a part of an idea.

"Stan, do any of the gods or Fates have the ability to open one of these portals?"

"I wouldn't know why not," he said. "It's similar to the power needed to slip between a moment in time. I've never tried it since I have no desire to meet myself in another dimension."

Suddenly I was confused again.

"Are you saying that the dimension to our left has never been attacked by these things?"

"No, it would take you moving over thousands of millions of billions of dimensions to find one that was never attacked. Think of a river. Every time there is a new event, it splits off two dimensions, like two almost-identical branches of the same river. When you all saved Lady Luck from the Bookkeepers' little mistake, you created two dimensions, this one where you saved her, and one where you didn't. So since the last attack on Atlantis, billions of new timelines have formed to the left of this one."

"Every major event creates a new timeline, a new dimension?" Patty asked. "Every event? Anywhere?"

My head hurt.

"That's right," Stan said. "If we stop these things this time, there will be a new dimension where we don't stop them. And in that timeline over, those of us existing in the neighboring dimension will have to fight them. And so on. The Fuzzy-Wuzzy need to keep eating, thus their need and ability to keep moving from dimension to dimension and eating entire populations. There are a lot of dimensions out there."

"I'm really sorry I asked that question," I said.

"I am sorry you asked it as well," The Smoke said. "But we must focus on this dimension and let the others fight their own fights."

At that moment Madge brought the milkshakes. She had managed to wash her face, but still looked completely distraught.

"Any ideas?" she asked, sliding a vanilla milkshake in front of me.

"A couple," I said.

At that she brightened up. Then she turned to The Smoke. "It's going to be a minute on the hamburger. I had the grill turned off."

The Smoke's regular was a hamburger, almost rare, instead of a milkshake.

The Smoke nodded and said, "Pull up a chair."

"So what's the idea?" Stan asked.

"I need one more piece of information. When these things run out of human food, do they attack each other?"

He shrugged. "I honestly don't know. Let me find out about both questions."

He vanished, and then a moment later he and Lady Luck herself appeared back.

Lady Luck sat down in Stan's chair and Stan quickly pulled over another chair.

"So what are you thinking?" Laverne asked.

I took a deep breath and stared at the most frightening god that existed, as far as I was concerned. "We need to bluff the Fuzzy-Wuzzy into going to another dimension, one where they have already eaten us all. Stan says we can form these gates to other dimensions."

"Easily," she said. "We don't as a general rule."

"Can the portals be made to be one way?" I asked. The idea was starting to form and I was getting excited.

"They can be," Laverne said, looking puzzled.

"I asked Stan if these things ever got hungry enough to eat each other," I said, "and he went to ask you."

Wolfgang Sucker appeared in all his bright blue glory, standing beside the booth next to Stan, his onion breath covering us all instantly as his head turned slowly from side-to-side.

Madge jumped up and took a couple of steps back, the look of shock on her face very clear.

"They must eat every fifty years or they will turn on each other," Wolfgang said, his voice again like sandpaper on a hard surface. "It takes them almost a half year to form the portals."

"How long does it take us to form a portal?" I asked.

"Instantly," Laverne said.

"One more question," I said. "When they leave a dimension, do they leave anyone behind?"

"Nothing but a stripped planet with nothing alive remaining," Wolfgang said.

I smiled. This idea just might work if there wasn't something I didn't know.

"Can you form a portal to one hundred dimensions back along the line of the Fuzzy-Wuzzy conquests?"

"We can go back thousands of dimensions, but all the worlds would still be dead," the Searchlight said.

I nodded. "Okay, here's the idea. "Form a portal to one of the destroyed worlds a thousand worlds away, and put that portal directly over their portal and somehow seal the connection. You won't be blocking it. They just won't know they haven't arrived here yet."

Stan and Laverne were nodding so I went on. "That way when they come through their portal, trying to get to us, they instead end up in a dead dimension without their knowing it. We bluff them."

"Actually," Screamer asked, smiling, "why not divide them into a thousand different dead worlds over a thousand dimensions, so far back they will only be able to eat themselves?"

Laverne stared at me for a moment, her dark eyes seeming to cut through me like I didn't exist. Then she said softly, "That might work."

At the same instant she and Stan and the Searchlight vanished.

Patty squeezed my hand and Screamer and The Smoke just smiled.

"You guys are really something," Madge said, shaking her head. "Milkshakes are on me."

I just hoped my idea worked and this wasn't going to be my last milkshake ever.

# FIVE

Forty-eight hours later, I stood with Stan, Patty, Screamer, The Smoke, and Wolfgang Sucker in a "you can't see us" bubble around the portal forming in the driveway to the MGM Grand Hotel valet parking.

Around us, Las Vegas went on with its normal, noisy life. The night air was warm, but thankfully not hot.

I was the one holding the "can't-see-us" bubble. Up until yesterday I didn't know I had that power.

Stan, with help from the Searchlight, and with energy support from all of us, had formed a dimensional portal that fit tightly over the Fuzzy-Wuzzy's portal. Stan's portal shifted the Fuzzy-Wuzzy almost a thousand dimensions back.

From what I understood, the Fuzzy-Wuzzy could only move from one dimension to the next every half-year; so if this worked, it would take them hundreds and hundreds of years to get back. And since they would turn on each other to eat long before that, they might never make it back.

And we were splitting the entire invasion force up into a thousand parts over thousands of dead dimensions.

All over the planet right now, Searchlights and gods were forming dimensional portals over the Fuzzy-Wuzzy portals.

It was our only plan of defense, and it had been my idea. I just hoped it worked. I hadn't slept, worrying about it.

If this plan didn't work, we were all going to be the first appetizer for a very hungry horde of bugs.

"Five, four, three," Patty said, counting down.

All of us poured energy to Stan as we had practiced, while the Searchlight held the connection between the two portals.

Since I wasn't a god, I couldn't see the forming Fuzzy-Wuzzy portal until suddenly it formed directly under the one Stan had formed.

A blur of black seemed to fill the opening of the portal. It went on and on and on.

And then nothing.

"I think they have all gone through," Stan said, beads of sweat forming on his face.

Suddenly the dimensional portal formed by the Fuzzy-Wuzzy closed and Stan slumped to the ground, breathing hard.

"I hate those bugs," he said, panting.

For a moment the Searchlight stood there, then he said, with his rough voice loud enough to hear even against all the noise of a Las Vegas night:

"It has worked."

Then he turned to all of us as Stan climbed back to his feet.

Suddenly Wolfgang Sucker's head stopped moving, and his blue eyes stared directly at us.

"This great battle will be shown on the heads of a thousand of my brothers for centuries to come. It has been my honor to be a member of your team, Poker Boy."

With that he vanished.

"Well, you all did it again," Laverne said from directly behind me.

We all spun to face Lady Luck.

She was smiling, and when Lady Luck smiles on you, you know it.

"Someday we might have to start paying all of you if this keeps up."

She laughed at her own joke, since superheroes don't get paid.

Then she winked at Stan. "Teach him how to jump through space, would you? I worry about him taking so many airplane flights."

Then she got serious. "Thank you. Every one of you. It was a perfect bluff, and a perfect idea. I just wish you all had been around in Atlantis' time."

With that she vanished.

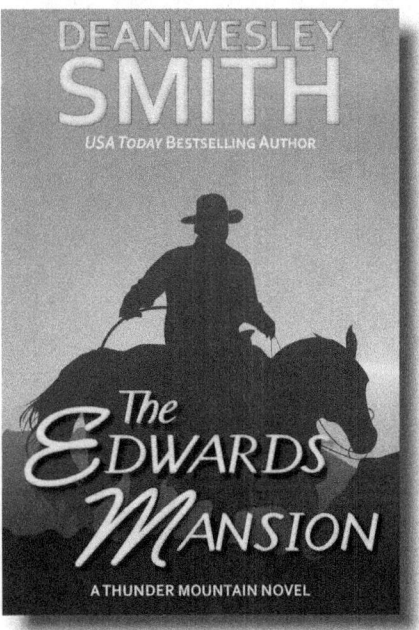

Stan turned to me, smiling. "Well done, as usual."

I didn't know what to say. I was so stunned that my idea had worked, I just sort of felt nothing.

"Milkshakes are on me," Stan said. Then he smiled even larger, "If you can get us there, Poker Boy, without calling a cab."

And suddenly I knew how to jump through space, from one location to another. I don't know how I knew, but I just did.

"That's a deal," I said. I took Patty's hand in mine and said to Stan, "Race you."

An instant later, I had my team sitting in our regular booth in The Diner as a fraction of a second later Stan appeared, still smiling.

Wow, that felt good.

Patty just squeezed my hand and smiled. Then she whispered in my ear, "Now we can see a lot more of each other."

I liked that idea. I liked it a lot.

The sound of crashing glass made us all turn around as one.

Madge was dancing on the counter in front of the kitchen. She seemed to be doing dance moves not thought of in years, and considering she always wore slacks three sizes too tight, it wasn't a scene that any sane person could watch for very long.

Stan started laughing and The Smoke just covered his eyes.

After a moment, all of us started laughing.

"Why not?" Screamer asked, and got up and started dancing as well, quickly joining Madge on the countertop.

"Looks like milkshakes are going to be a minute," I said between huge laughs of relief.

"Thanks to all of you," Stan said, "we have the time to wait."

~

# Now Available
## from all your favorite booksellers in trade paper and electronic editions.

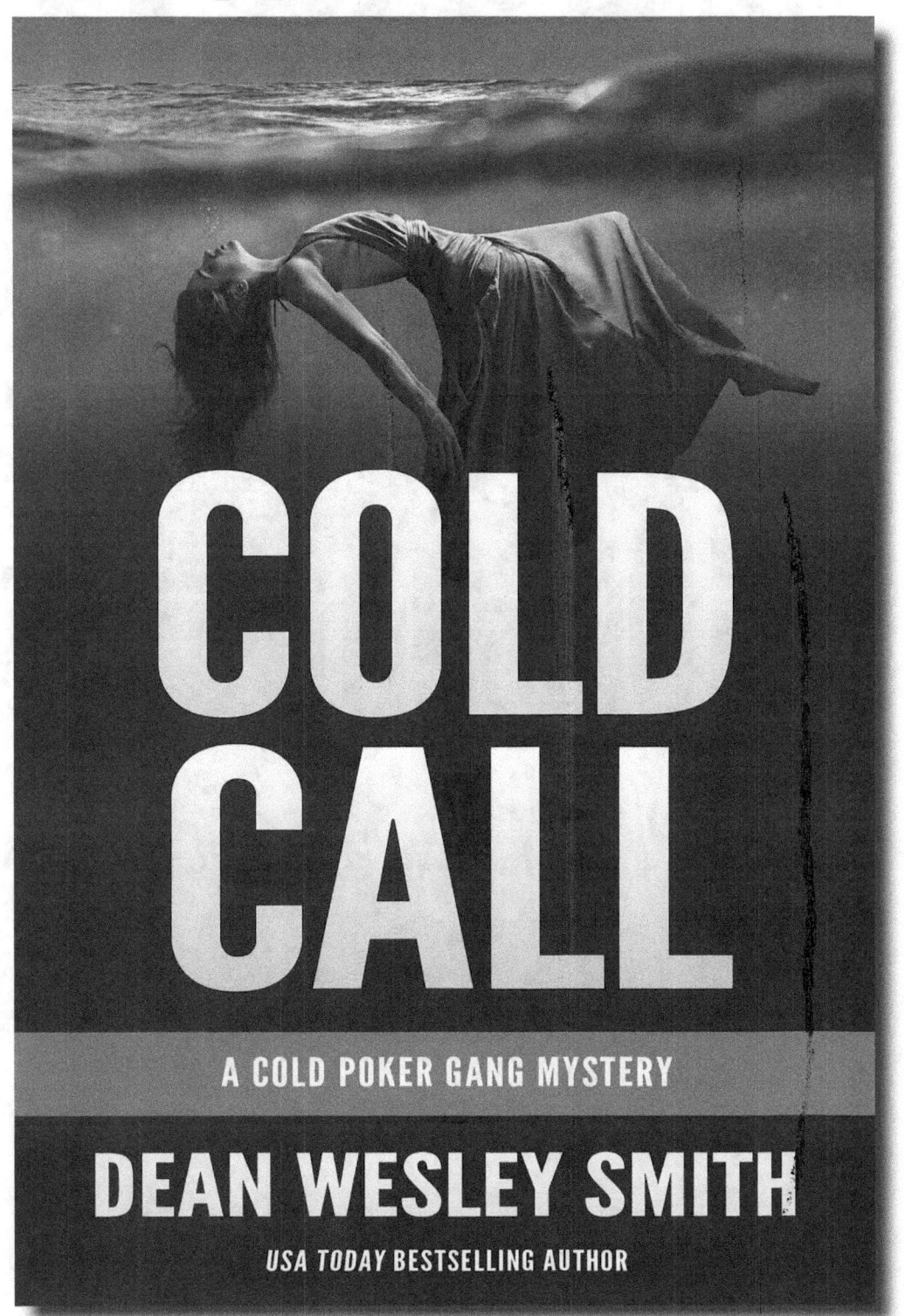

Dean Wesley Smith

*USA Today* Bestselling Writer

A Crime Story
of Love and Movies

HUSBAND
DUMMIES

*When two couples decide to play the Bob and Carol and Ted and Alice pretend game, things take a nasty turn for the worse.*

*Especially when the wives want to change the movie.*

*A very strange crime story with a movie twist.*

# HUSBAND DUMMIES

## ONE

**"WHY IN THE WORLD** does anyone live in this god-forsaken humidity?"

My words drifted through the thick air with no wind to take it away. Two midwestern natives—used to this thick, water-filled air—sat next to me in the drainage culvert under the concrete bridge as above us trucks thundered over, swimming through the thick air down I-70. The two men ignored my question without even pretending not to hear it.

Bob-from-Minnesota, my husband and a real jerk, just shook his head and stared at the ground, blood dripping down his arm. It had already soaked his white T-shirt, mixing with the sweat-stains growing under his arms. It looked like a lot, but it wasn't that much blood loss. He had just dislocated his shoulder and had a few surface wounds. I figured it served him right for being such a screw-up. And the worst driver I had ever seen, especially for a getaway car driver.

I wanted to just slap him, but instead I sat on the ground with my back against the rough concrete side of the culvert and just sweated. Humidity had to be one hundred percent in this tunnel. Why hadn't I planned this robbery for October instead of August?

Ted, Bob's best friend, adjusted his Cub's baseball cap and then pulled the shoelace from his right dress shoe free and flipped it away. He had twisted his ankle so badly in the getaway that his foot was too swollen to even stay in his shoes. His blue dress shirt was soaked with sweat, turning it even darker, and his usually perfectly combed brown hair was messed up and had a weed caught in it.

He was going to live as well. None of us were injured enough to die.

My two men, my two lovers, sat across the small space from me. Both looked a mess, more than any morning-after hang-over look, and I had seen both of them like that. Hell, I had seen those two in just about every position possible and to be honest, I was sick of it. Jail time might actually be a relief.

As bad as they looked, I had to admit, I wasn't doing much better. The getaway from my perfectly planned bank robbery had turned sour, ending up in a car wreck because my stupid husband somehow forgot how to drive. I was so angry I could hardly think. I just hadn't expected Bob to screw things up that way. It had sure changed my plans in a hurry.

And Alice's plans as well. She was Ted's wife and my best friend. We had left her stuck in the car, shouting at us to get out and run before the cops got there. She wasn't actually stuck, but the men didn't know that. Alice was just flowing with the changes in my plan caused by my dear husband's bad driving.

Alice had a body men lusted after, wore clothes that were always in perfect style, and bought the best jewelry. I just hoped she was better at getting out of that

van and getting away than Bob was at driving it.

Now, because of his bad driving, the three of us were all injured. I figured I had a broken arm. I had tucked the arm inside my white blouse and downed four Advil from my now long-lost purse to hold back most of the pain. Sitting still, the pain just throbbed and I could ignore it.

Amazing the things I could just ignore. I was a master at it.

That didn't much matter at this point. I couldn't ignore the fact that, more than likely, the only place I was going was to jail, thanks to Bob's awful driving. Sitting under the freeway in a drainage ditch in the middle of midwestern farmland didn't offer us much chance of escape without a miracle and I didn't expect that.

I hoped for it for myself, but didn't expect it.

But one thing was for sure, I wasn't going to make the miracle happen just sitting in this culvert. I had to get moving.

"I'm going to go up and jump in front of a speeding truck," Ted said. "Get this over with."

"Don't," Bob said. "We'll be out in four years; three if we behave."

"Alice might be dead," Ted said. "Shot by the police or something."

"She's not dead," Bob said, his voice firm. "Besides, Carol here can handle us both, can't you, baby?"

"Screw you," I said. "Ted, Alice is just fine. And I'm going to be glad to go to jail just to get away from you two."

"So, brilliant master-planner," Bob said, staring at me. "What do we do next?"

I stared back, wondering what the hell I ever saw in the guy. Sure, he was good in bed, knew how to make me come more times than a doorbell being pushed by a bill collector. And he was damn good-looking. But he was also a real wimp and a really bad driver. How the hell had I ended up marrying a shitty-driving jerk with no courage?

"We give up," I said. "Go up and sit on the edge of the road until some lame-ass cop comes and arrests us. At least they'll get us out of this heat."

I managed to move my broken arm enough to get a look at my watch. It was about time to hope for the miracle. Past time, actually. I needed to move.

"And then what do we do?" Bob asked, being his usual annoying, snide self. Snideness and humidity just didn't mix. Nothing mixed with heat and humidity as far as I was concerned.

"Serve our sentences and get back together after we're out," I said, doing my best not to sneer at him.

"Brilliant!" Bob said. "Wish I could think that well."

"Screw you," I said.

"Children," Ted said, pushing himself up and balancing on his one good foot while leaning against the concrete wall of the culvert, "After this wonderful conversation, I think I'll face that truck grille now. Someone want to help me up there?"

"Sure," Bob said, standing and moving to get under his best friend's arm. "But don't expect me to push you. I'm not doing time for murder as well."

"You know," I said, "I'm beginning to hate both of you as much as this heat."

# TWO

**I TRIED TO PUSH** myself to my feet, but the sharp pain from my broken arm took my breath away and made me stop. I sat there, staring at the ground, trying to cram the pain down and into a place I could just ignore it. I needed to move, to keep going, and I couldn't let some pain stop me.

"You going to make it, babe?" Bob asked, actual concern in his wimp-ass voice.

"Yeah." I took a deep breath, gritted everything in my body that I could grit, and stood.

Damn, that hurt.

Damn my arm.

Damn my stupid-ass husband.

The heat seemed to get even worse, if that was possible. I was sweating so bad, I had a small river running down between my breasts and into my crotch.

I used my good hand to brace my bad arm up tight under my breasts and keep it from moving as much as possible, then nodded to my husband. "Let's go."

"Well, this was sure fun while it lasted," Bob said, smiling at me.

"It was," Ted said.

"Except it didn't end like this in the movie," I said. "Make sure you give the cops your real names."

"Yeah," Bob said, smiling. "Less bad press if we don't get known as the Bad-Sex Bandits."

"And we're worried about press coverage now?" Ted asked, shaking his head. "I'm getting more and more serious about facing the grille of that speeding truck."

"Who said the sex was bad?" I asked.

"All right," Bob said. "The Good-Sex Bandits. You happy?"

"Purring like a drowning kitten." I took a step and let the pain wave wash over me, braced my broken arm even tighter and kept going toward the opening of the ditch.

Bob and Ted stumbled over the uneven dirt behind me, both men grunting from the pain of the movement. During the sex play between the four of us, I loved to listen to them grunt in unison as they pounded me or Alice. Now it sounded just sad, especially echoing between the sounds of the cars and trucks overhead.

Damn I hoped Alice was all right. Imitating that old movie wasn't such a bright idea in hindsight. Bob and Carol and Ted and Alice. We even took their names and it became such a fun game, such a major part of our lives, that I now thought of my husband Danny as Bob. If we had just left the fun with the sex and the names and the games, we'd have all been fine. But no, we had to come up with a foolproof plan to get rich, move to the Bahamas and live the good life forever as Bob and Carol and Ted and Alice. None of us liked how the movie ended, so we figured we could change it.

Well, this was sure ending much worse.

Now, if a miracle didn't happen, it would be years of jail ahead of me without Bob or Ted and especially Alice. Every movie had to end, I guess. I just wished it wouldn't end like this.

This ending sucked. Unless I got my miracle and Alice had done her part of the plan.

I stopped and wiped the sweat out of my eyes. Who the hell lives in this kind of humidity? I wanted to go back to Southern California so bad I could taste it. Now that wasn't going to happen for years, either, thanks to Bob's shitty driving.

I stopped and rested in the hot, glaring sunshine outside of the culvert, waiting for the two men to catch up. Bob had lost a lot of blood and Ted looked white from the pain. As I had figured, I doubted either

of them could make it up the twenty-foot bank to the edge of the highway.

"You two stay back in the shade," I said. "I'll climb up and get the police."

"You sure, Babe?" Bob asked.

"As sure as I'm ever going to be," I said.

I turned my back on the two men I had slept with and slowly started to climb. The nightmare of just a simple movement was almost too much for me to keep going.

Twice I slipped and had to stop as the jarring pain blinded me and took my breath away. Getting to a jail and a hospital would be a relief after this.

I stumbled up onto the edge of the hot freeway and glanced back at my husband and Ted. They were nowhere to be seen. They had done as I had told them and moved back into that hot culvert to sit and wait.

What wimps. What did I ever see in those two men?

# THREE

**CARS FLASHED PAST,** then a big truck, kicking up a hard wind filled with fine sand.

There wasn't a cop in sight.

Good.

Suddenly, in the other lane, a blue camper braked hard, swerved to the inside lane and then off the road and across the shallow ditch between the two sides of the freeway. It hesitated for just a moment to let a big truck flash past, then spinning dirt and dust, it accelerated toward me, cutting across the two lanes and sliding to a halt off the freeway near me.

Alice.

Right on time. My miracle had arrived.

And, I hoped, with all the money.

"I thought I'd never find you," Alice said as she jumped out of the camper and ran toward me. "I've been cruising this freeway for the past half-hour looking for you."

I didn't quite stop her from hugging me, a wonderful, sweaty hug that almost caused me to pass out from the pain in my arm.

"Oh, man, are you all right?" Alice asked, stepping back.

"Bob broke my arm in that stupid wreck. It took a little longer to get everything set up."

"And where are the two love machines?" Alice asked.

"Down in the ditch right under us," I said. "Both hurt, but not that seriously. They just think they are. A couple of wimps."

Alice nodded. "Nothing new there."

"They thought you were captured."

"And we're going to be," Alice said, her control voice in full force, "if you don't get into the camper before too many more people see you."

I didn't argue.

The first movie was over. Bob and Carol and Ted and Alice was rolling the credits now.

But we just hadn't bothered to tell our dear husbands that this was a double feature. Thanks to Bob's shitty driving, though, we still had a few twists and turns to make it through.

The camper Alice had found was one of those small things with a small back bedroom, another bed or storage area over the driver, a tiny kitchen area, and a bathroom so small, you couldn't sit down without scarring your knees.

It looked new, so new in fact that it had a price and features list glued to the counter.

I knew exactly where she had gotten it, which dealer lot, which dealer, and how. I had planned it, and it seemed that Alice had carried out my plans perfectly, even after the wreck.

Alice slammed the door and scampered into the driver's seat. The van was still running and I could feel the air-conditioning flowing over my sweating face and arms. Between the pain, the excitement of being rescued instead of arrested, and the air-conditioning on my skin, I almost had an orgasm right there.

I moved to the copilot chair as Alice kicked the van into gear, waited for traffic to speed past, then got onto the freeway. The movement of the camper and the roughness of the road forced me to again hold my broken arm tight up under my breasts.

"I'm going to need a doctor to set this before we go too far."

Alice nodded. "So do I. That husband of yours sure can't drive."

It was at that moment I noticed the dried blood and the bandage wrapped around her leg.

"You got any idea of where we might find one?" I asked as I turned both dashboard vents to face me, blowing cold, wonderful air over my skin.

"If you can make it, I have an old friend who's a doctor about six hours south of here. He'll help us if we give him a little side treat, if you know what I mean?"

"After a shower, that will be a pleasure."

Alice laughed. "Better than what old Bob and Ted are going to get. You feel bad about them?"

"Are you kidding?" I asked. I didn't feel bad in the slightest. Relieved, actually, to be away from them.

Alice laughed. "Yeah, know what you mean. When should we tell the police where they are at?"

I smiled at the idea of the two of them coming up out of that culvert to find the police waiting and me not there. "Let's give them a half hour to sweat."

"Good," Alice said. "We'll be across the state line by then as well."

"And the money?"

Alice nodded toward the back. "More than we're ever going to be able to spend, tucked safely under the bed in the back."

All I could do was laugh. Except for the car wreck, the plan had gone perfectly. The only robbers the bank saw were Bob and Ted, and no amount of talking on their part was ever going to convince anyone that their wives had taken part. In fact, with the blood that I splattered around our house before we left, it's going to look like the two of them killed us and dumped our bodies before their little bank robbery.

I braced my arm and sat back, enjoying the cool air and the smooth ride of the camper. Alice and I had money, and we were free.

Completely free.

With new identities already made up and set.

Judy Freeman, a.k.a. Carol, wife of Bob was now dead. Welcome to the world Thelma Downer, rich widow of oil tycoon Bobbie Downer.

I closed my eyes and just let myself relax.

"Carol, you all right?"

"Carol's dead," I said, glancing at the woman I loved more than anything in the world. "Remember?"

Alice laughed. "That's right. The new movie starts now, doesn't it?"

"That it does, Louise."

She smiled as I turned to face her. "So, after the doctor, where would you like to go, Thelma?"

"Anywhere but the Grand Canyon."

~

***First Three Cold Poker Gang Novels***
***Available at your favorite booksellers.***

# Now Available
## from all your favorite booksellers
## in trade paper and electronic editions.

*USA TODAY* BESTSELLING AUTHOR
# DEAN WESLEY
# SMITH

## A DOC HILL THRILLER

# DEAD MONEY

""[An] exhilarating political poker thriller."
—*Midwest Book Reviews*

# Dean Wesley Smith

*USA Today* Bestselling Writer

**A Jukebox Story**

# A GOLDEN DREAM

*Sometimes very special friends, even friends you can't remember, give you a chance to change your past by following the memory of a special song.*

*Should you take the special Christmas gift, take the trip, and change your own history?*

*Or maybe take a look at tomorrow and change that instead.*

*"A Golden Dream" was first published under the title "The Song of a Gift Horse" in* Black Cats and Broken Mirrors *anthology edited by Martin H. Greenberg and John Helfers.*

*A very altered version of this story was part of the novel* Melody Ridge: A Thunder Mountain Novel.

# A GOLDEN DREAM
## *A Jukebox Story*

## ONE

**SHE CAME THROUGH** the heavy front door of the old hotel with a face as young as yesterday. And for just a moment the stale piss-smell of the thick air, the stained and faded linoleum floors, the peeling paint on the smoke-yellowed walls were forgotten by the three of us in the front foyer.

For just a moment we forgot our long, dull days of old men's boredom, moving like zombies from our rooms, to the sitting room with the television, to the front stoop, back to the sitting room, then back to our rooms, punctuated only by a silent lunch and an even more silent dinner in the small kitchen.

Mitchel, Hank and me. When she came through that door we forgot we were three corpses too damn old to just lie down and be done with it. We forgot we were the last residents of The Golden Dream Hotel for men.

We even forgot it was Christmas Eve.

A year ago crusty Jamison bought the old hotel from a development agency. We all had an understanding that the four of us would be able to live in the hotel until we all died. Jamison died the next month at the age of sixty-eight, giving me the hotel in his will. Now all the three of us did was sit around and wonder who would be next. But no one talked about it. Since I am the youngest at sixty-six, I figured I would have the longest to wait. Since I owned the place that sort of made sense.

And now, as she stood there on this cold winter evening, her short, perfect-skinned nose wrinkling at the smell of old age, even the thought of dying was forgotten.

She blinked in the dim light and then focused on the old black and white television flickering in the corner. I could see she had bright, large eyes, thick eyebrows, and a full mouth. The kind of mouth I remembered that Alice had back what seemed like a million years ago. Alice was my first love, my first sexual partner, my first real girlfriend. We never married and I always wondered why.

The young woman brushed a long slender hand against her nose, then straightened her shoulders as if she were going to face a firing squad. She stepped toward the three of us. Her high heels clicked on the linoleum floor and I wondered when that floor had last felt the steps of a woman.

"Excuse me," she said. Her clear, soft voice seemed to fill the old hotel with life. She stopped and glanced around, as if startled by the sound of her own words. "I'm.... I am looking for a Mister Fred Thorpe."

I thought I was going to swallow my teeth. She was looking for me, as if I actually existed to someone outside of these walls besides the social security department. "That's me," I said, sort of waving a hand in her direction. My voice sounded really odd following hers.

She seemed relieved and took another step toward me. "Would it be possible for us to talk?"

I shrugged and pointed to the vacant chair that had been Jamison's.

She shook her head. "In private, if you don't mind."

Again I shrugged and without looking at the others pushed myself up from my chair in the most dignified manner I had managed in years. I nodded toward the hall that led past the old front desk cage. "We can talk back in the kitchen."

She said fine and I shuffled ahead of her distinct and firm footsteps down the hall and into the kitchen.

After we were both settled at the old wood table she took a deep breath. She started out saying that I wasn't going to believe her.

She was right.

I didn't.

# TWO

**THE OLD WURLITZER** jukebox sat like a king at the end of the oak bar in the Garden Lounge. Radley Stout, the owner of the Garden polished the old jukebox every week and the chrome and glass sparkled as if the machine had a life and energy of its own.

Above the jukebox was a polished wood and glass case that held four drinking glasses with the old Garden Lounge logo and a name etched on each.

Carl, Dave, Jess, and Fred.

Except for Christmas Eve, the jukebox was always unplugged and the glass case always locked.

The Garden Lounge was a local, quiet bar. It had old-styled booths, a hundred regular customers and enough atmosphere in plants and low lighting that everyone felt safe when they came in.

Radley Stout had owned the bar for eleven years and for ten Christmas Eves he had plugged in the jukebox. Tonight was to be the eleventh and he hoped it would be something special.

# THREE

**THE KITCHEN** smelled of the hot dogs we had had for lunch, and the dirty pan and plates were still in the sink. I couldn't remember if it had been my turn to do dishes or Hank's. It was Christmas Eve. What did it matter?

"My name is Sandy Reeves," the good-looking young woman said to me across the kitchen table. "I am a private investigator and I was hired to find you by a Mr. Radley Stout."

I laughed and leaned toward the woman who looked like she might be barely old enough to be out of high school. "Right. So what is the gimmick? What are you selling?"

She didn't seem bothered by my rude question at all. Calmly she reached into her large purse and pulled out at small, black pistol. With a thump she placed it on the table between us. "I have a permit for that," she said, smiling slightly.

All I could do was stare at the black gun while she pulled her wallet out of her purse, flipped it open, and slid it across the table at me. Then she scooped the gun back into her purse.

Open in front of me was her driver's license and her private investigator's license from the state. I glanced at her birth date. She was twenty-six. At lot younger than any child Alice and I might have had. I nodded and slid her wallet back at her. "So what does this Mr. Stout want from me?"

She sort of shrugged. "Actually, I am not exactly sure. He owns a place called the Garden Lounge, down on Main. He said he just wanted to buy you a Christmas Eve drink."

"That's all?" I shook my head. "He hired a private investigator to find me to buy me a drink?"

She nodded, almost looking embarrassed. "I am just supposed to take you down to the Garden Lounge. And Mr. Stout gave me strict instructions to not force you in any way. He knows nothing about how you are living or even that you are alive. So are you interested in having a drink?"

I glanced at her and then around at the old kitchen and the dishes in the sink. It was Christmas Eve and I had absolutely nothing better to do. "What the hell," I said. "I've always believed that you never look a gift horse in the mouth."

"True," she said. "You just never know when a miracle might happen."

I stared at her, but she only smiled, not explaining at all. Slowly I pushed myself back from the table and stood. "I could use a drink tonight."

She nodded. "So could I."

# FOUR

**JUKEBOXES,** by their very nature, are time machines.

Not only do they look as if they belong in another decade, but by playing songs, they sometimes take the listeners back to the memories associated with those songs.

The jukebox in the Garden Lounge did a little more than that. It physically took the listener back to their memory from a song. And the listener could be there, inside the listener's younger body, until the song finished.

The listener could also change events that occurred during the time the song was playing. And by changing those events, change the future.

That was what made the jukebox so dangerous. That was also the reason the jukebox was never plugged in. When new customers in the Garden asked about the jukebox, Stout just told them it was broken.

Stout, the owner and only bartender of the Garden Lounge, originally saved the old jukebox from the bankruptcy court a good hour before the bank locked up his first bar. For one full year in which he had tried to run the bar, the jukebox had sat in the back hall, covered with a blanket and a good inch of dust and grime. It had been just part of the old furniture and things that came with the bar. Almost as a lark, he took the jukebox to his garage, hiding it from the bank, figuring that he would fix it up some day.

That day came another year later on a Saturday.

He was thinking about buying a second bar and giving the bar business another try. The old jukebox would make a great item to have in the new place if he could get the jukebox to work.

When he opened the jukebox up, he found a lot of sealed boxes and weird looking electronics that seemed far beyond anything needed or standard in an old Wurlitzer jukebox.

He studied the insides for a few hours without figuring any of it out. Finally he just dusted everything off, fixed the electrical cord that looked as if someone had ripped it from the back, and plugged the jukebox in.

The jukebox blinked a few times, the colored lights came on, and nothing blew up.

So Radley went in search of a record to play on it. Luck would have it that the only forty-five record Radley owned was an old song he and Jenny had bought. It was their song and it reminded him of the day in the student union that he wanted to ask Jenny to stay with him, not leave town, but hadn't. The next day she went back to college and eventually met another man.

He dug the old record out of his scrapbook, cleaned it off, put it on A-1, and punched the buttons. With the first note the world shifted, his garage disappeared, and he suddenly found himself sitting in the old Student Union café, facing Jenny across a scarred table.

The air in the room felt warm and seemed to close in on him. He could smell Jenny's wonderful perfume. Her light brown hair was pulled back and off her face. She was nodding in time with the beat of the song, waiting for me to say something.

And smiling. Night after night for years Radley had remembered, and would remember, that smile.

The chair felt hot and sticky under him and his hands seemed to be glued to the table top. The song, their song, was on, echoing through the large room, and he stared around at the others studying or eating at tables nearby before turning to stare at Jenny. He could not believe this. He could remember all of his older memories and his younger ones, too. He knew exactly that he wanted to ask her to stay with him, maybe even marry him.

And he knew exactly what his future held because he hadn't.

The thought of that future scared him even more than asking her to stay with him.

He sat there, not saying a word, staring at Jenny and her smile until the song ended and he found himself back in his garage. He took a deep shuddering breath and then barely made it to the back door before he threw up.

The next day, after a long night of no sleep, he finally got up the courage to play the record again.

And again he did nothing but sit across from Jenny and stare.

He never played their song again, even though it remained for eleven years as A-1 on the jukebox.

Except on Christmas Eve.

On Christmas Eve, the only night he plugged in the jukebox for his friends, he takes that special record off and places it in the safe. He didn't want to ever take a chance of anyone else playing it.

# FIVE

**SANDY REEVES,** Miss Private Eye with the Big Black Gun, held the front door of the Garden Lounge open for me to shuffle through. I had passed by the Garden a hundred times and always thought about stopping. Never had. It had just not been the right time. I never expected Christmas Eve to be that right time.

The place smelled of smoke and green plants and I immediately felt at home. Much more than at the hotel.

Empty tables cluttered the center of the room and booths filled both side walls. Christmas candles were lit on every table. An old-looking polished-wood bar filled the wall opposite the front door and three men sat on stools near the bar's center with their backs to the door. They were the only three customers. A medium-sized man in a white apron was standing behind the bar and when I came through the door he looked up and said, "Holy Shit."

The three men at the bar turned around as if pulled by the same string and the bartender put a glass on the bar and headed around the end to meet me.

He dodged around a few tables with ease and we met in the middle of the bar. He grabbed my hand and shook it as if we were old friends seeing each other again after many years.

I studied his face as he stared at mine. He looked to be in his early fifties, with thinning gray and brown hair. His eyes were green and his smile seemed to fill his entire face.

After what seemed like a long moment he took a breath and sort of shook himself. "I'm sorry. I'm Radley Stout. I own this place. And I'm really glad you came."

All I could do was shrug. "Not as if I had much else to do," I said. "And you did offer a free drink."

He just laughed and patted me on the back. "Come on up to the bar. I have a few friends I want you to meet."

I took the stool on the left of the three men and the lady P.I. took the open stool to their right.

Radley Stout went around behind the bar as he did the introductions. Dave was the closest to me. He was an airline pilot and his daughter was the private investigator who had found me. Next to him was a big guy named Carl who did construction and beside him was a convict-looking man by the name of Billy. I nodded at them without really noting what any of them looked like, then turned to Radley Stout.

"All right," I said. "Why bring me here?"

Again Stout laughed. "As you said, to have a Christmas drink. Give me a moment and I will explain."

He rummaged in the drawer under the cash register and came up with a key. Then he went to the end of the bar and unlocked a glass case that was mounted on the wall over an old jukebox.

Everyone at the bar watched in silence as he pulled out three of the four glasses that were in there and walked back to the sink in front of us. He rinsed out one of the glasses and held it up for me to see.

It was a crystal-type glass, with the Garden Lounge logo etched near the center and the name Fred over the logo.

"So you needed a Fred to join the toast this year. That it?"

Stout shook his head, set the glass down on the mat above the ice and started to rinse out the other glasses. "No, actually that glass was yours eleven years ago."

No one else said a word. They either watched Stout wash the glasses, or they stared down into their own drink, as if slightly uneasy about something.

I had never seen that glass before and had never met Stout before or been in this bar before. This gift horse was starting to look like a bust, just as most of them had in my life. I laughed for a short moment and then said, "Not highly likely."

"That's true," Dave said from beside me. "It isn't highly likely. But I think it's true."

I turned to Dave. He was a clean-cut sort, with short hair and wrinkles on his forehead that cut lines across his tanned skin. "Were you there when I supposedly owned that glass?" I pointed in the direction of Stout and the glass. He had just finished washing out a glass that had the name Dave over the logo.

"In a manner of speaking," Dave said. "I was. But I too do not remember the first time. However, I do remember the second."

I just stared at him for a moment before shaking my head and pushing myself back off my stool. Free drink or not, this was just a little too much. "I knew this entire thing was crazy, but you folks are all a bunch of loonies."

Stout put the third glass on the rubber mat. It had the name Carl etched on it. "Fred. Please just hold on for a moment. I just want to buy you a drink and tell you a story. I know you won't believe me, but what can it hurt? It's Christmas Eve."

Sandy looked down the bar at me and sort of smiled. "I told you that you wouldn't believe this."

I stopped with one hand still holding onto the back of the bar stool and looked down the line of faces staring at me. It seemed clear that everyone wanted me to stay and everyone was taking this craziness very, very seriously. I took a deep breath and let it out in a noisy sigh.

Sandy laughed. "You said never look a gift horse in the mouth. So stop looking."

At that I laughed. "All right. One drink and then Miss Private Investigator there can take me back."

"And a story, too," Stout said. "Don't forget."

I nodded and climbed back up on the stool. "A story too. As long as you don't want me to buy anything."

Stout nodded and smiled. "I promise. Now what would you like to drink?"

I ordered a vodka tonic and for the next half hour the conversation was light and fun. I could feel the heaviness and gloom of the Golden Dream Hotel lifting from my shoulders as everyone laughed and talked and sipped their drinks. There seemed to be a friendship among these people that I had not felt before. A closeness that went far beyond customers in a bar.

I ended up asking for a second drink and Stout refilled my special glass. As he placed it on the napkin in front of me he said, "I think it's time for the story."

Everyone nodded as Stout went back to stand in front of the well where he was sipping on a glass of eggnog. He leaned against the backbar and raised his glass. "First, a toast. To friends again united."

I drank to the toast not knowing what he was talking about. I assumed the united friend he was talking about was me, but since I had never met the man before, that was going to be some story.

"I had the Garden for just over a year," Stout said. "And I had some really good, regular customers. But four of those customers had become my good friends. Dave. Carl. You, Fred. And Jess." With each name Stout tipped his drink in the person's direction. With the last name he tipped it in the direction of the glass case that still held one glass over the jukebox. I assumed the name on that glass was Jess.

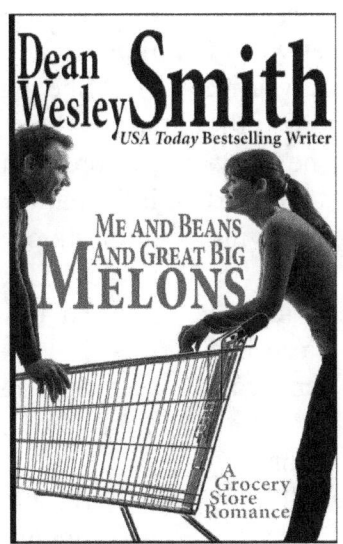

"Fred," Stout said, "you see that jukebox there?" I nodded as he went on. "Everyone here except you knows just how special that jukebox is. This is the part of the story that you will not believe no matter how hard or well I explain it, so just think of this part as fiction. All right?"

Again, I just nodded, so he went on. "That jukebox can take a person back to a memory. Not just in your mind, but in real flesh and blood. It's a sort of time machine."

"Fiction is right," I said and Stout just held up his hand.

"I discovered how the jukebox worked by accident before I ever opened the Garden. Ten years ago on Christmas Eve I decided I would give my four friends a chance to go back into their pasts. A special Christmas present from me. At that time you were divorced from a woman by the name of Alice and you had two kids."

Suddenly the bar felt very warm. He was assuming that I had been a regular in here for almost a year and once been married to Alice. But I knew that wasn't true. I must have had too much to drink with just two drinks, since it felt as if the room was spinning. How could he know about Alice? And he was saying that I had married her and divorced her after having two kids.

Stout was watching me and after I looked up at him he went on. "You had been divorced from Alice for ten years and you hated her. Completely and totally hated her. It was a standing joke among the five of us. You also had a daughter by the name of Jenny."

"So what happened to her in this crazy world of yours?" I asked. My voice had more anger in it than I could remember.

Stout just shrugged. "I assume she was never born. When you left here through the jukebox, you said the song reminded you of the night you and Alice first made love. The night you conceived Jenny which forced you two to get married out of high school."

Again the room felt too warm. The night Alice and I first made love was the night her parents were gone to a Christmas party. Right before going over to her house, I had gone to the drugstore to buy some rubbers. I remember almost chickening out and then the next thing I knew I had a pack of them in my hand and was heading out of the store. Alice and I always used one every time we made love. She met another guy a year later and left me because she said I was never going to ask her to marry me. She was right. I never did.

"You all right?" Stout asked. I glanced up. He had moved down the bar and was standing in front of me. Everyone was looking at me. I tried to laugh, but it sounded sort of weak, even to me. "You did your research real well. Sandy there must be a really good investigator."

"She's good all right," Stout said and Sandy held up her glass in a thank-you gesture. "But she didn't find any of this information out. I knew about Alice and your divorce because you told us over and over for almost a year."

"So how come I didn't live any of this?"

Stout just sighed. "Because you lived a different life after you changed whatever it was you changed that evening. The only reason I remember you is because I was touching the jukebox when the song ended. For some reason that allows me to remember the old timeline. I remember you being in here, but no one else does."

He pointed at the glass in front of me. "I was holding onto the glass, too, when you didn't come back."

"Didn't come back? What do you mean I didn't come back?" Again I was trying to keep the anger out of my voice. But all of this was making me mad. And damn tired.

"You changed something while you were back there. And whatever you changed did not lead you to the Garden again in your new life. At least not until now. If you had not changed anything, you would have come back when the song ended."

Dave was nodding beside me. "That happens every year to me. This year I plan to go back and watch Sandy being born. It will be a Christmas present to myself. Trust me, I will be very careful to not change anything."

I looked at Dave for a moment and then shook my head. "So why bring me back here now. Assuming that all this is true, which I find not likely, why now?"

Now it was Stout's turn to look slightly embarrassed. "I guess I just wanted the old group back together again on Christmas Eve. Selfish, I guess."

"Looks like you didn't pull it off," I said. "What about that other glass? Didn't your P.I. there find the guy?"

Stout took a sip of his eggnog and then looked up at me. I could see the pain in his eyes and the sadness that coated his face. The silence in the bar seemed to fill the room with a thick, heavy feel. "Sandy found him all right," Stout said. "He changed something, also, when he went back that Christmas Eve ten years ago. In the new world he created he was killed by a drunk driver. We found him up in Memorial Cemetery."

I shook my head in disbelief and looked down at my name in the old glass. "So what did I do in the previous life? Be a lawyer or something?"

Stout took a deep breath and then laughed. "Not hardly. You worked for the

*Some Classic Dean Wesley Smith Stories*
*Available at your favorite booksellers.*

city. I think you had something to do with streets or something like that."

It was my turn to laugh. "I did that in this life, too. Fancy that. So how come, if that machine can change someone's past, you just don't go back and stop that guy from getting killed?"

Stout shook his head. "I am actually glad it doesn't work that way. Way too much responsibility. No, you can only go back to your own memories. You can't change other people's memories. Or their lives."

Dave stood. "Tell you what, Stout. Plug in that jukebox and I will go watch my daughter being born. That might just give old Fred here a new outlook on life."

Stout shrugged and walked down the length of the bar to the jukebox. Dave downed the last of his drink and joined him.

"You got the record I brought on there?" Dave asked as Stout reached around behind the jukebox and plugged it in. The colored lights flickered for a moment and then held steady. It was a beautiful old Wurlitzer, with the chrome arch, red, green and blue colored lights, and bright red buttons. Inside I could see the disk full of forty-five records all waiting to be played.

"Just punch up old B-4," Stout said and handed Dave a quarter.

Everyone at the bar had swung around on their stools and were watching intently. I felt uneasy and nervous, even though I knew the only thing that would happen was that the song would start playing and that would be that.

Dave dropped the quarter into the slot, punched the two buttons and then stood back as the machine clicked and whirred. Inside I could see a record being picked up and placed on the turntable.

Stout saluted Dave.

"Don't go changing anything, Dad," Sandy said. I want to be here when you get back."

Dave laughed. "Don't worry. Just going to watch."

The jukebox clicked and the song started. I recognized it immediately. An old Rick Nelson song called, "It's Up To You." That song reminded me of...

The bar shifted and was gone. For a quick instant I felt dizzy and then everything went black.

And then came back to a bright white spotlight. Right in my eyes.

# SIX

**"GOD DAMN IT!"** Stout shouted as the song started. Sandy, Billy, and Carl had all been looking at Dave and Stout. But as one they turned to look at the bar stool where a moment before Fred had been sitting.

"Oh, no," big Carl said.

Sandy just shook her head. "Every year we do this and every year something weird happens."

Stout moved down the bar and put his hand on Fred's bar stool, as if that would help bring him back. "Damn it! I forgot to ask him if he had a memory with that song. What the hell was I thinking?"

"Don't worry about it, Stout." Sandy said. "He'll be back."

Stout picked up Fred's glass and looked at the name. "He didn't come back last time he left here through the jukebox." Stout reached over and picked up Dave's glass. Then he headed back for the jukebox. "I want everyone holding onto the jukebox when the song ends.

If he doesn't come back this time, I want someone besides me remembering him."

Sandy laughed. "Boy won't Dad be in for a surprise when he gets back."

# SEVEN

**WHEN A SPOTLIGHT** hits you square in the eyes, your first instinct is to raise your arm to cover your face. And that is what I did. Only my arm hit the steering wheel of my '57 Chevy.

"What...?" I said out loud as I glanced around like a frightened deer caught in a hunter's sights.

The car's engine and lights were off and the windows were rolled up tight. Rick Nelson belted out the song on the radio. Sweat trickled down the side of my face and down my bare chest. The temperature inside the car must have been that of a steam bath and the spotlight was coming through the fogged-up front window.

"Oh, no!" A young woman's voice said from beside me and I turned to look at her. That was when the memories flooded in like light pouring through an open door between a dark room and a lit one.

Marcy was struggling to get her bra back on. We had dated for two years after Alice left me. She worked at the department store downtown in the men's section and wanted me to be her husband more than almost anything. That fact had suited me just fine because it made parking with her a lot of fun. She ended up marrying a guy from the appliance section of the store and had three kids last I heard.

Tonight was our first anniversary of going out and we were parked on the canal bank behind the orchard to the south of town. It was the only night we ever got caught parking by the police.

"This can't be," I said. I looked completely around the car. It was my '57 Chevy all right. The one I wrecked in 1969 while driving drunk on New Year's Eve. A moment ago I was sitting in the Garden Lounge with a bunch of people who I thought were nuts and now I was back here parking with Marcy.

I held onto the steering wheel with sweaty hands. I could still freshly remember getting here and what Marcy and I had been doing just a few short moments ago. I remembered taking her bra off and almost putting my hand up her skirt. In fact I was still aroused from all of it and I hadn't had anything but a piss-erection in years back at the old Golden Dream Hotel.

I had said I never looked a gift horse in the mouth. The Private Investigator's words now echoed back through my mind: "You just never know when a miracle might happen."

So this was what she was talking about.

Marcy smacked my arm. "Hurry! Get your shirt on."

Outside I heard the car door close and a vague shape through the fogged window started toward the door. I had a clear memory that we had gotten dressed before the cop got to the window and he let us go with a strict warning to be moving along. We had laughed about it for days.

Stout had warned Dave not to change anything when he punched up the song. And he said that the reason I didn't end up back at the Garden was because I changed something when I did this music/time-travel thing the last time.

If what Stout had been saying back there at the Garden was true, and it looked like it was, I had better do some fast dressing.

Real fast.

Marcy was already buttoning her blouse as I turned around and grabbed my shirt off the back seat where my younger self had tossed it a short time before. I had it on and buttoned, in what seemed like impossible speed to my sixty-two-year-old brain, just as the cop tapped on the window.

Marcy straightened her hair as I rolled down the window and looked into the cop's flashlight. "Wow, that's bright."

I remembered that was the exact same thing I had said when I didn't have sixty years of memories to draw upon.

The cop shined his light on me, then on Marcy.

She smiled at him.

I turned and smiled at him.

Then Ricky Nelson stopped singing.

And I was back on my bar stool at the Garden Lounge.

Stout, Sandy, Carl, and Billy stood around the jukebox, touching it.

Dave stood in front of the jukebox staring at them.

"Wow," was all I could say.

All four cheered and Stout held up my empty glass as if in a toast.

It felt really good to be back.

# EIGHT

**I HAD ANOTHER DRINK** as I told them about my adventure with Marcy, getting caught parking, and who she was to me and my life now. I explained that my two years with Marcy had mostly been trying to forget about being in love with Alice. It was a fun time, but nothing really important, or life altering.

After I got done telling my story, and Dave told his about how great it was to watch his daughter being born, Sandy went back through the jukebox to visit her senior prom. She came back smiling and laughing and told us all about it, right down to where she and her girlfriends spiked the punch to get the guys drunk.

I remembered in my time that the guys were the ones who put booze in the punch. Things do change.

Carl went back to visit his mother and when he came back he didn't say much and no one really pushed him.

It shocked me both times when they just sort of popped out of existence and then back again when the song ended. And before each song Stout asked me if I had any memories associated with the song.

Stout and Billy both declined to play a song, so when Carl returned and dropped back onto his bar stool, Stout moved down the bar and stood in front of me.

"Usually," he said, "we only go back once, but since your first trip was an accident, are you interested in giving it another try this year?"

His question surprised me, for some reason. "Give me just a second to think about it." I slid my glass toward him. "How about a refill?"

He nodded and moved down the bar with my glass as I thought about Alice. She had turned out to be the one woman, over all the years, that I truly loved. Now Stout was giving me a chance to go see her again. And maybe tell her how I really felt. Maybe keep her from leaving me.

He was offering me another gift. And this was a very special gift.

I turned on my stool and looked out over the empty Garden Lounge. This evening had been one of the nicest, and wildest, I had spent in more years than I cared to remember. I enjoyed the people and I enjoyed the place.

Why leave it at the moment?

Besides, if Stout was right, Alice and I ended up in a really ugly divorce that I hated enough to change once. Maybe I was just cut out in this life to live alone, as I had done. Maybe on this gift, this year, it was better to look the old horse in the mouth.

Stout set the glass on the napkin and I turned around to face him again. "Thanks for the offer," I said. "But I think I will pass this year. One was enough. Maybe next year if you want me back."

Stout broke into a huge smile. "Every year. You are always welcome."

He moved down the bar and unplugged the jukebox. "That's it for another year," he said.

We all toasted the jukebox and then we spent the next hour laughing and talking about anything and everything, including what Stout could remember of my previous life, including how really unhappy I had been with Alice.

At a little after midnight on Christmas morning, Sandy dropped me off in front of the Golden Dream Hotel for Men.

I almost bounded up the front stairs, feeling younger and more alive than I had in years. I'm not sure why a few drinks and a trip into my own past would make me feel that way. But it did.

And for the moment that was all that mattered.

I unlocked the front door and went into the front foyer.

The place was dark, the only light the one over the old front desk cage. Hank and Mitchell were long asleep. In fact this was the latest I had stayed up in years.

I looked around at the deep shadows and the worn furniture. It was as if I was seeing it for the first time. Seeing the age and the stagnation. Nothing had changed in this room for as long as I had lived here.

I patted the back of Hank's chair and a small cloud of dust rose in the dim light. Maybe it was time to bring some life back here.

I wandered over to the open area beside the cage and looked up at the high ceiling. Twenty feet, maybe. More than enough room for a Christmas tree.

Tomorrow the three of us would stop down at the Garden to have a Christmas drink with Stout. He had promised he would fix us his special eggnog. And then we would go buy a Christmas tree for the hotel. It was time we started a few traditions of our own. The guys would piss and moan, but they would enjoy it.

And then maybe the following week I might find an old jukebox. A real one that only gave you memories instead of trips through time.

You didn't always have to go into the past to change the present. As I discovered tonight, with a very special gift from the strangest gift horse I had ever met, sometimes you can do it right now.

~

# DEAN WESLEY SMITH

# AN EASY SHOT

## A GOLF THRILLER

*In the first installments, Seattle Police Detectives Bonnie and Craig, while taking a late night walk on a Scottsdale Arizona golf course, happen to overhear a conversation between two men plotting to kill a United States Senator.*

*At the same time, a young golf professional's wife is kidnapped. Scheduled to play with the Senator, he must do what they ask or his wife will die.*

*Bonnie and Craig get the FBI and local police involved. Everything is set and they play with the Senator to help protect him.*

*Nothing goes wrong, but that night, they see the two men again who they had overheard.*

*Now, the next morning, starting the second round of golf, everyone waits and watches.*

*A horrific accident on the golf course almost kills the Senator, but he is fine and sent on to Washington while they set a trap for the man coming to kill Danny, the young golf professional.*

*The man is killed in the hotel room by Craig and an FBI agent.*

# AN EASY SHOT

## Part 6 of 8

## CHAPTER SEVENTEEN

*Sunday, April 9th*
*7:01 p.m.*

**BONNIE HAD BEEN** a cop long enough to see her share of death. And every time she hoped she would never have to see more.

This time was no different.

Just easier.

The deaths of children and teenagers were the ones that bothered her the most, but every death seemed to carve a small chunk out of her soul, leaving her feeling just a little more empty and a little more jaded toward life and people.

Having the guy die in the fight in the hotel room was startling, and disturbing, but for some reason she didn't find herself that upset about it. He had tried to kill Senator Knight, had kidnapped Danny's wife, and was more than likely going to kill Danny and his wife if they had given him time.

Having him die wasn't a great loss to the world, the way she figured it. She knew that was cold, but sometimes being a cop made you cold when it came to scum.

Craig clearly felt the same way. Craig seemed more upset that he was going to have to do massive paperwork and attend post-shooting hearings after all this was over. Hagar had promised him he would help speed the process. And if he did have to come back for a hearing, just think of the golf he could play. That comment had cheered Craig up some.

Right now she and Craig and the rest were much more worried about getting Danny's wife recovered safely. The cell phone they had gotten off the dead guy was stolen, and the number called had been to another stolen cell phone.

No surprise there.

Maxwell and his team had managed to get the area the cell call went into narrowed down to a ten-block radius in a Phoenix suburb. But the only way to pinpoint the call exactly to one location was to call the number again.

And somehow keep the line open long enough to get a fix on the location.

With the help of the Scottsdale police, the Phoenix police, and other agencies nearby, they had quietly blocked off the entire ten-block area and were standing ready to swarm in on the location as soon as they had it pinpointed. There was going to be no talking with whoever was holding Danny's wife. They were going to swarm in and take her back without warning.

Danny seemed ready as well to help in getting his wife to safety. They had all gone back up to the FBI's room on the top floor of the hotel, leaving Danny's room for the crime scene people and FBI to go over. Maxwell had figured if Danny made the phone call, there might be more of a chance of it staying connected long enough to get an exact location pinpointed.

Bonnie agreed and was standing beside Danny, with Craig on the other side, when Maxwell said, "Ready."

Danny nodded and pressed redial on the dead man's cell phone. Then he carefully put it to his ear as if he was afraid it might explode on him.

Bonnie forced herself to let out the breath she was holding and put her hand gently on Danny's shoulder to let him know they were there for him.

After a short moment Danny said, "The guy said I could talk to my wife again."

A slight pause.

Danny looked panicked.

"He's right here," Danny said. "Just put my wife on."

Behind Danny, Maxwell signaled thumbs up.

They had the location and were closing in. But he wanted Danny to keep talking if he could. It would be better for those moving in to keep the guy on the line and busy somehow.

"All right, all right," Danny said. "You can talk to him. Then let me talk to my wife again will ya?"

Bonnie was impressed at the young pro. He had played it perfectly.

Danny glanced at Bonnie with the phone held out in front of him. He had the questioning look of what was he supposed to do now? He had gone through all his lines they had worked on and he clearly wasn't capable of making something up in his state of mind.

Craig motioned for Danny to talk into the phone again, but Bonnie could tell Danny was clearly about to lose it. This was all far, far beyond his depth.

Bonnie shook her head at her husband, signaling him to not push the young pro any more.

Craig glanced at Maxwell, then took the phone. He smiled at her and gave her his nothing-to-lose-shrug.

She agreed. They had pinpointed the location and at this point they had nothing to lose and everything to gain by keeping whoever was on the other end of the line busy for just a few more seconds.

"Let him talk to his wife, fer cryin' out loud," Craig said.

Bonnie was impressed. Craig's voice sounded like a passable imitation of the dead-man's voice. Sometimes her husband's hidden skills were just amazing.

"Yeah, yeah, I know," Craig said after a short moment, "but the kid wouldn't budge without another call."

Suddenly Craig held the phone away from his ear. Bonnie could hear the sounds of gunfire coming from the phone. One shot, another two quick ones, then nothing.

Craig carefully put the cell phone back up to his ear and listened for a moment, then shook his head that there was nothing on the other end.

They all looked at Maxwell.

"Is Steph all right?" Danny asked Maxwell.

He said nothing.

Bonnie could feel her stomach clamping down hard as she waited. Beside her Danny seemed as if he might just faint from the fear and worry and waiting.

Maxwell was listening to reports from his people on headphones. Suddenly he broke into a big smile at Danny. "They have her."

"She's all right?" Danny asked, his voice weak and shaking.

"She's all right," Maxwell said, smiling the broadest grin Bonnie could have imagined the man smiling. "They're taking her to the hospital. You can meet her there."

At that Danny just slumped into a chair and broke down and started crying.

For a moment the hardened cops and agents in the room looked at the young golf pro with stunned looks.

Then Bonnie sat down beside him and put her arm on his shoulder for comfort. He deserved a good cry.

Around her a lot of men were smiling, including her husband. It looked like this was over for the moment.

And for a change, real life had a happy ending, even if the guy was crying.

# CHAPTER EIGHTEEN

*Sunday, April 9th*
*8:37 p.m.*

**THE MAN CHARLES** Robins called Bill signaled for the limo driver to stop in a parking lot as he checked the account balance on his laptop computer screen one more time just to make sure.

It came up the same.

Charles Robins had shorted him exactly a half million dollars on the final payment.

"Stupid idiot," the man said.

He snapped the computer closed and put it back in its case.

Then as he was looking out the window of the limo, he started to laugh. "Stupid men always make stupid mistakes."

He had always known that Charles Robins was a stupid man, so this final act of greed was no surprise. It was mostly luck and underhanded dealings that had allowed Robins to build his house-of-cards fortune. The man had known that before he went to work for Robins. For years he had waited for this exact moment, the exact right opportunity to strike at Robins, take as much of Robins's money as he could, and move on.

He had gotten a half million out of the idiot. And now Robins had made the fatal mistake of not paying the rest. It was time to show Robins that there were some things not even an idiot could buy his way out of.

The man signaled for the driver to start up again, then reached into a briefcase and pulled out a cell phone. It was one of ten stolen for this operation that he hadn't used yet.

He punched in the number for the man he called Benny. The guy was all New York and proud of it. Benny didn't know the man's real name and he didn't know Benny's. They simply helped each other out when help was needed.

The phone rang three times too many without being picked up.

The man instantly clicked off his phone and punched the button for the window beside him to roll down. He used a handkerchief to carefully wipe off his fingerprints from the phone and the keypad. There was a stretch of empty desert and litter a few hundred feet ahead. As the limo went past he tossed the phone into the litter beside the road.

He put the window up and then keyed in the intercom to the driver of the limo. "Turn right at the next corner and then right again at the next and head back into town."

"Understood, sir," the driver said.

He sat back and thought. Was it possible that Benny had just put the phone down? By this time of night he should have already been at the house with Danny the golf pro. And both Danny and his young wife should be dead, if Benny followed orders. He was hoping to make use of the two bodies.

Was it possible that Benny was busy with that chore?

The man nodded and pulled out another cell phone. He punched in another number, this one for the phone of Benny's assistant who had been guarding the young wife.

The phone rang two too many rings before a voice answered. "Yeah."

The voice sounded like Benny's voice, but it wasn't Benny.

He clicked the cell phone closed, quickly wiped it clean of his fingerprints, and tossed it out the window. It bounced under a parked car.

"Driver, take a left at the next corner and go until you reach the freeway. Then head for Tucson."

"Yes, sir," the driver said.

It was clear that Benny and one of his men were either dead or captured by the FBI. It made sense that they would get the young pro to break the moment the

Senator had his accident. And from there the trail was easy to Benny and his helper. He was going to miss Benny, that was for sure. A good worker.

But he wasn't going to miss the money he now didn't have to pay Benny. That was an extra bonus.

But what to do about Charles Robins?

The man sat back in the comfort of the limo and sipped a brandy, thinking. He wasn't halfway to Tucson before he came up with a great plan.

# CHAPTER NINETEEN

*Sunday, April 9th*
*11:21 p.m.*

**CRAIG PUSHED AWAY** his mostly empty plate and sipped on the Diet Coke. They had been lucky to find a place with food this good so late on a Sunday night. It looked more like a diner stuffed inside an old freight warehouse, but Hagar had sworn by the place and he had been right. Great service, great food, and background music low enough to talk over.

What more could they have asked for?

At the moment Hagar was finishing a large plate of some sort of Mexican food Craig didn't recognize.

Maxwell had already pushed away the last of his barbecue chicken.

Bonnie was trying to polish off the last few pieces of her steak.

Around them there were still people coming in and being seated. Clearly the locals knew this place well. Craig couldn't imagine how busy it was during peak hours if there were this many people here on a late Sunday night.

For all of them it had been one very long day, topped with the scene in the hospital with Danny and Steph getting back together. Just the memory of that made Craig smile. The quiet, sullen young golf pro that they had played golf with all weekend suddenly had become happy, full of life, with a light in his eyes as he and his wife hugged and cried together.

Craig couldn't even imagine playing golf while Bonnie was being held hostage. But Danny had done what he thought he had to do. And somehow had managed. He was one strong kid.

From what Maxwell had said, because of Danny's help getting to some of the men behind the attempt on the Senator's life, and the situation of his wife being kidnapped, no charges against Danny would be brought. He and Steph were just victims of the larger plan.

At the hospital Craig had apologized to Danny for treating him so roughly on the cart path after the accident.

Danny said it was all right. For not calling the police at once he deserved much more than that. Then he had added that he never wanted to ever be on the receiving end of being arrested again by an angry cop. Once was enough.

Initially Craig and Bonnie had been scheduled to fly out early in the morning and be back to work on Tuesday from this so-called vacation. But since Craig had been involved in the shooting of one of the suspects, there were going to be hearings to attend and paperwork to fill out.

Bonnie had called the airline and pushed their flight back to Tuesday. Then she had told their bosses in Seattle what had happened. So with an extra day or so, maybe, just maybe, they could end up having a little time alone.

"So what happens next?" Bonnie asked Maxwell as she gave up and pushed her plate away from her with a few bites of steak still left.

Maxwell shrugged. "Steph Baines said there were three men who kidnapped her. Two are now dead, so we still got one out there somewhere."

"The guy who made the phone calls to the cell phones?" Craig asked.

Craig's attempt to imitate one of the dead men on the second call had failed instantly. Clearly the man making the calls was smart and was being very careful. Both calls had been made from different stolen cell phones, and both phones had been quickly found, obviously tossed out of a moving car.

"More than likely he's the third," Maxwell said, nodding as he sipped a cup of coffee. "And he's now a good distance out of the area."

"But he wasn't the money man," Hagar said.

"I doubt it," Maxwell said. "We're pretty sure that is Robins. He's the only one with motive to hurt the Senator. But proving it without the third man in custody is going to be damned hard."

"Money trail?" Bonnie asked.

"Maybe," Maxwell said. "If we can get the warrants, and if he was just plain stupid."

Craig could only nod his agreement. He doubted Robins was that stupid.

"Is the Senator safely in Washington?" Bonnie asked, her voice low so only the four of them could hear the question.

"Safe and ready for a press conference right before he goes in for the vote tomorrow morning," Maxwell said, smiling. "All his close family and friends have been informed of the ruse so they won't worry."

"Even without being caught it seems that Robins is going to get his just desserts," Craig said. "I'd love to see his face as he watches that press conference."

All of them laughed and agreed.

Craig glanced at Hagar. "When are you going to want me in the station tomorrow morning?"

Hagar looked at his watch. "How about at the crack of noon?"

"Perfect," Craig said, feeling relieved that Hagar hadn't said eight. "Just over twelve hours of vacation."

"A good night's sleep," Bonnie said, sighing. "Won't that be a change for this trip?"

"Let me know what it feels like," Maxwell said.

"Yeah, me too," Hagar agreed.

Thirty minutes later Hagar dropped them off in front of the hotel and twenty minutes after that they were in their swimming suits and sitting in the bubbling water of the hotel's massive hot tub.

The tub was located in a corner of the swimming pool area. It was surrounded by boulders and made to look more like a natural hot springs than a hotel hot tub. Craig had to admit that was a nice touch. And the best part was that when sitting down in the tub, the boulders blocked the view of the pool and the hotel, leaving nothing but the rocky mountainside above the hotel and the night stars. It made for a wonderful relaxing hot dip in what felt like a mountain pool.

They were alone in the hot tub since it was almost one in the morning, but another couple was sitting on the far side of the pool, holding hands and talking while their feet dangled in the water.

"Perfect temperature," Bonnie said, letting her body float with the bubbles beside him. "A great meal and a hot soak. I think I needed this."

"I couldn't agree more," he said, leaning back and letting the warm water soothe his nerves. "Only one thing I need more than this and sleep."

She laughed. "And just what might that be?"

Without looking at her he said, "You have to ask?"

Her hand moved over and rested on his crotch. "What do you have in mind?"

"Maybe an hour of sex in that big bed upstairs," he said, "then eight hours of sleep, then another hour of sex tomorrow morning."

"Before or after breakfast?" she asked.

"On second thought," he said, "maybe both."

"Oh, feeling young, are we?"

"What are vacations for?"

She laughed as her hand moved slowly on him for a moment and he hardened under her touch.

Then she said, "That's a perfect plan if you add in just one thing."

"Trust me," he said, "the thing you're playing with is part of the plan."

She laughed again, but didn't stop moving her hand. "No, I just wanted to stay in the hot tub for a few more minutes. Let some of the tension drain away."

"Before we go back to the room and create more tension?" he asked.

"Exactly," she said.

Maybe, just maybe, they might be able to salvage this vacation after all.

*To be continued...*

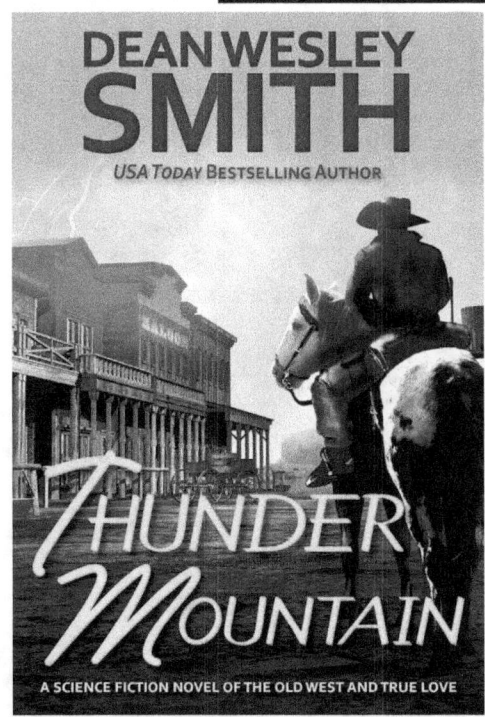

## The First Two Thunder Mountain Novels
### Available at your favorite booksellers.

# Dean Wesley Smith

*USA Today* **Bestselling Writer**

# Last Car for this Time

## A THUNDER MOUNTAIN STORY

*When men start getting run over by slow-moving train cars in a gold rush town in the mountains of Idaho, Marshal Duster Kendal must solve the murders.*

*But there might not be a motive besides the fact that Duster Kendal lives.*

*Duster knows exactly what to do about that.*

*And he needs to do it fast before things get much, much worse.*

*An early story of when Bonnie and Duster were first testing time travel and a problem they had early on.*

# LAST CAR FOR THIS TIME
## *A Thunder Mountain Story*

## ONE

**MARSHAL "DUSTER" KENDAL** really had no great desire to see the death scene. He stepped off the wooden porch of the Dewey Hotel and moved his six-foot frame as slow as he could down the dry dirt of the Main Street of the tiny town of Dewey, Idaho. With each step his boots kicked up a small cloud into the hot, morning air.

Lately he'd seen far too many deaths and he had a hunch this one wouldn't look much different than the other two he'd seen here and others he'd seen over the last year.

Things seemed to be unraveling. He knew the signs.

This time he had met the dead guy two nights before in the Benson Saloon in Silver City. It was one thing to see a body of a stranger. Another to look on the dead face of a man Duster had watched pour drinks for two hours.

The morning sun beat down through the clear August sky with such force Duster could almost feel it like a weight on his shoulders, pressing him down into the dirt of the street. The day would be a scorcher before it was finished.

People thought him odd to wear his light, oilcloth duster even on hot summer days, but he had learned while in the Arizona territory a long, long time ago that it actually kept him cooler in the hot sun. His wide-brimmed Texas cowhand hat kept the sun off his face as well.

Wearing the long, brown coat had gotten him the nickname "Duster" and he had no intention of changing that now. He actually had grown to like the name and the coat. Both fit him like a comfortable old pair of boots.

He wore his gray and brown hair long and streaming out the back of his hat to cover his neck, and his face and chiseled features gave away very little of his actual age, which was north of forty-five now. Only his bright green eyes let his intelligence shine through and he was known for the intensity of his gaze. Sometimes he could stare a man down enough to kill a growing problem.

Today he had no plan on being out in the sun much longer than he needed. If this death followed the pattern of the others, he wouldn't need to be out long.

And this morning just maybe he might figure out what was causing these men to die.

Or at least why.

He had a hunch he knew, and with no train due back in the valley for six days, he had time to find out if his hunch was right and set everything on the correct path again.

In his years of wearing a badge, he'd never seen anything quite like this. Of course, no place else in the west, or in the world for that matter, was like the Owyhee Mountains. They had been mostly ignored by the huge rush on the Oregon Trail close by in the 1860s and if it hadn't been for the gold found in the streams and deep veins here, Duster doubted anyone would be in this hostile place.

And if no one had come here, he wouldn't be here either.

These deaths by train were the reason he was up here from Boise in the mining district of Silver City. The only law in the valley was a constable in Silver City named Ben and his deputy. The poor guy had called for help after the first death. Ben's job was to break up bar fights, not figure out why someone died under the wheels of a train.

What bothered Duster even more was that there didn't seem to be anything going on in the town that would cause this. No fights beyond drunken brawls, no mine-labor disputes beyond normal. Yet four men in three weeks had been run over by slow-moving freight trains just down the hill from Dewey, Idaho.

Dewey was a silver-and-gold-mining boomtown tucked in the bottom of a valley leading up between War Eagle and Florida Mountains in the Owyhee Mountain Range in Southern Idaho. The town straddled Jordon Creek like it couldn't decide which way to step.

The main attraction of the town beside the huge twenty-stamp ore mill and the Blaine tunnel was the Dewey Hotel. Colonel Dewey had built the hotel tucked up against the west side of the narrow valley. Two stories and as plush as anything Duster had seen in San Francisco or back east. Colonel Dewey himself lived in a large house beside the hotel and seemed just as upset at all the deaths as everyone.

Maybe more. Colonel Dewey had brought in the railroad in the first place. He knew that if the deaths didn't stop soon, there wouldn't be a person left in the valley to work his mines. This was scaring everyone and Colonel Dewey had offered Duster extra to solve this fast.

Duster had turned him down, of course.

If Colonel Dewey actually knew how fantastically rich Duster was, and where he actually came from, he would have never offered. But Duster played the role of marshal well, even though he always stayed in the best hotels when he traveled and only ate at the best restaurants and drank the finest brandy.

Duster felt that just because he worked as a marshal didn't mean he couldn't fully live life as well. And no one really questioned the money he spent and he didn't offer an explanation.

The railroad had put a spur line up the valley to the Dewey Mill in 1881. All the ore from Silver City and all the mines farther up either had to be hauled out over forty miles by wagon down to Murphy or taken the short three miles down to Dewey in the summer months when the train could get up the valley. In a few months the snow would start flying and the train wouldn't return until late spring.

If it returned then.

The town of Dewey was dying. Duster had seen it before around the west. Towns sprang up and then vanished, often within years. In a hundred plus years there wouldn't be anything left here but a bend in the road.

Silver City, the county seat three miles up Jordon Creek above Dewey, wasn't in much better shape. He had no doubt that the winter would kill most everything in this valley and the mines that were marginal wouldn't open again. And after the snow started flying the train wouldn't be back.

Plus, with the Bank of California going down a few years back and payrolls for most of the mines in this area being lost, people were already not trusting anyone.

The valley had a few more generations in it as it slowly died, but not much beyond that.

And now the deaths of four good men weren't helping.

This area was about to go down and would become a ghost town.

Duster just needed to figure out why people kept dying under the wheels of slow-moving ore cars so he could get back to his wonderful suite in the luxurious Boise Hotel.

He really wanted to get back to the life he had picked and the restaurants and the women in Boise as well. Everyone knew how Duster loved his food, and his friends wondered how he could eat so much and stay so rail thin. He had his secrets he would say.

Duster had a lot of secrets.

# TWO

**DUSTER KEPT TRUDGING** down the street thinking about the deaths. None of this made a lick of sense. If someone wanted to drive people out of the valley ahead of when they would naturally leave, what would they gain besides changing the natural history of this valley? The mines were pinching off. The death of this valley was only a matter of time, so these deaths couldn't be about that.

Duster walked past the big mill and down the rail line to where a group of bystanders gathered near the edge of the almost-dry creek across from the tracks.

Just as with the others before, this body wasn't a pretty sight.

The head and upper torso were on one side of the track, the waist and legs on the other. The train had pretty much cut old Benny in half, leaving his toes pointing down and a stunned look on Benny's face as he stared with blank eyes at the morning sky.

Benny had to be at least fifty and his face and hands showed many rough years in the mines.

The blood had stained the rock fill around the ties slightly darker than normal for about ten feet along the track. No telling which stains were Benny's and which were from the other three men. All of them had died in the same place.

The train had left parts of Benny's guts strung out along the rail. That smelled just downright awful, like an overfull outhouse baking in the afternoon heat. The nasty odor had kept the gawkers back a distance. And the hot morning sun wasn't helping matters.

Duster had no desire or need to go any closer, so he stopped about twenty paces away and just studied the scene. He knew what he would find if he went in closer. Nothing.

The same as every man who had died before Benny in the same spot in the same way.

Benny wouldn't have a mark on him. And no ropes had held him in place under the train. And the railroad men wouldn't have seen him on the tracks when they walked the train before starting down the valley.

Somehow Benny had gotten under the car on the tracks in broad daylight just as the train started.

And without anyone seeing him.

Then he had turned face up and let the train cut him in half.

What a horrid way to die.

Duster shook his head and turned to look at the silent crowd.

"Marshal," one man said, fear clearly in his eyes. And some anger as well. "When is the great Duster Kendal going to stop this?"

"Yeah," another guy said. "I got a family that's starting to get spooked."

"They should have gotten worried after the first one," Duster said, glaring at the man. "Someone wants all of us to be scared. Seems to me it's working just fine."

Duster watched the faces of the twenty people, watched their eyes in the hot sun. Not a one of them seemed satisfied at what he had said. All showed fear.

Damn. He shook his head and turned away from the crowd. It would have been too easy to have the murderer standing around watching. He hadn't been in the crowd at the previous murder either and that had been larger. This was happening so often now, fewer and fewer people were going out to look and stand in the odor of a man's guts cut open and baking in the hot sun.

Duster turned and headed back up the road toward the hotel and the bar there. He had four men to meet and if luck held, they would have his answer.

He just didn't want to hear what he was afraid it might be.

This all might be his fault.

# THREE

**THE AIR FELT** cooler inside the hotel and out of the hot sun.

Duster pulled off his hat and coat and carried them into the bar over his left arm, his right arm free to reach for his gun on his hip. Over the decades he had become one of the most accurate shots with a Colt around. Luckily, he seldom had to use that skill.

The bar smelled of cigar smoke and a faint odor of puke. None of the windows were open yet, trying to hold off the heat of the day as long as possible.

The four men were sitting at the bar, clearly drinking and not talking, their heads down. He motioned for them to follow him and he went out and into the dining room and to a large table in the back.

The dining room was even cooler since the drapes were pulled closed and it still smelled of the breakfast bacon. It was empty.

Bonnie, a middle-aged woman with a bright smile and bright red hair, saw him coming and got up from where she was reading the Silver Avalanche paper. Her blue dress had been protected from a couple of morning spills by a stained apron tied around her neck and her waist. Her wonderful brown eyes looked very, very worried.

She looked as good as always. He had known Bonnie for a very long time and every time he saw her, his heart skipped a beat. Being in love with Bonnie was a normal thing for him.

And lately he had been missing her a lot. More than he wanted to admit to even himself.

"Another one, Marshal?" she asked standing across the table from him, her smooth hands on the back of the chair.

Duster nodded. "Not anything you'd want to see."

She shook her head, worry and fear filling her eyes. "You think it might be against us?"

"It might be," Duster said, nodding. "I'm about to find out for sure. Could I get a big glass of water if you wouldn't

mind? Actually, make that two and add a couple chips of ice."

"Never a problem for you, Marshal," she said, smiling and turning as the four men followed him into the room carrying their drinks from the bar.

She would have to go down into the cellar to where they stored the ice from the winter, and it would cost him, but after that walk in the sun, it would be worth it.

And he tipped well. Everyone in the valley knew he tipped well. It got him a lot of extras he didn't even ask for.

Bonnie knew a lot more about him than that as well, but in public they stayed in their parts, their lives.

The four men pulled out chairs and sat at the table with him, their eyes down, trying to find the bottom of their shots of whiskey like there were answers there, clearly not liking what they had to report to him.

He had stationed the four men on the hillsides above the parked ore train, two on one hillside, two on the other. He had paid them all good money to stay out there from sunset last night until the train moved this morning. Where they had been on the hillsides, all four of them should have seen the death.

"So what happened?" Duster asked.

Not a word as all four stared at their drinks. These men were miners, rough men, strong men, able to handle the dangers of deep rock tunnels, yet all four were afraid to talk at that very moment.

He didn't blame them. They were good men, not men used to seeing things that they didn't understand. They had all seen death, he knew that. But how this death had happened they weren't used to seeing and that was what was bothering them.

They didn't think he would believe what they had seen and then be mad at them and maybe even blame them.

The silence in the dining room was broken by Bonnie coming back and bringing Duster his two large tumblers of ice water. The water was naturally cold from the spring up the hill above the hotel, but the ice made it even better.

"Thanks," he said to Bonnie, then took a long swig out of one. Then he pressed the sweating cold glass against his forehead.

That felt wonderful. It had been even hotter out there than he had thought.

He took a handkerchief from his pocket and wiped off his face, then took another drink.

All the while the four big miners sat silently, not even bothering to take a drink of their whisky shots.

"Well," he finally said as Bonnie moved back over to her paper. She could hear from there clearly, which was good. She would need to know if this was what he thought it was.

"You wouldn't believe us, Marshal," Dave Jennings said and the other three nodded, not looking up.

Duster decided to just let them off the hook. "Benny just appeared on the tracks, right before he was run over. No one put him there. Am I correct?"

All four of the miner's heads snapped up to look at him like he had lost a screw.

"That's right," Dave said. "One second he wasn't there and I thought nothing would happen and the next moment he was on the tracks and the train was running him through like so much soft butter on a hot day. That vision will haunt my dreams, let me tell ya, Marshal."

The other men nodded in agreement, clearly seeing again what had happened out there on those tracks.

"I was afraid of that," Duster said, sighing. Damn it all, he had just settled into a nice routine in Boise.

He glanced over at Bonnie who was just shaking her head as well. She knew they were in trouble.

He reached into his breast pocket and took out four gold coins, each coin the equivalent of two-week's work in the mines for these men. He had already paid them an equal amount for their night's watch, but now he had to buy their silence, let things get back to normal here.

He slid one coin each to the men. "This is to get you to forget what you saw and not mention it to anyone."

All four looked at him with a puzzled look.

"I don't think anyone would believe us even if we wanted to speak, Marshal," Dave said, picking up the coin and looking at it.

"There is another just like that for each of you if I don't hear a word of what you saw for the next month. Understand? Not even a rumor."

All four nodded.

Good, that would give things time to calm and change and be forgotten and winter would be that much closer by then.

"So where did that guy come from, Marshal?" Dave asked, his voice a whisper. "How'd he get under those wheels? Do you know?"

"Not exactly," Duster said, being truthful. "But thanks to you four, I now have a lead. Now not a word."

All four nodded, picked up their coins, and headed back for the bar. He didn't blame them for drinking after what they had just seen. It was bad enough a man had died like that. But just appearing out of thin air in that spot was something no sane man could grasp.

At least not someone from 1898.

After they had left, Bonnie came over and sat down beside him as he finished off his first glass of water and started on the second.

"We going up to the mine?" she asked.

"Looks like we have no choice," Duster said. "Things are twisting bad around here."

She sighed and looked around. "I was really starting to enjoy this timeline."

"Yeah, me too. But it's coming apart really fast," Duster said. He knew that the moment he arrived in Dewey and saw the ore train. In the real timeline, the original timeline, Colonel Dewey had never managed to get the spur line up Jordon Creek.

And those four men were still alive in 1898.

# FOUR

**AT MIDNIGHT,** Duster and Bonnie left the Silver Nugget in Silver City arm in arm. A couple people saw them and tipped their hats to them as they passed. This time was such a polite society. It was one of the many charms Duster liked about it.

They angled up the hill toward Florida Mountain to the west, following a wagon trail, pretending to just be out for a walk together under the spread of stars on the warm summer night.

The slight moon and the sky painted with stars was enough to let them see where they were walking. After they were a distance from the buildings of town,

they stopped talking and just walked in silence, her arm tucked into his left arm.

To Duster it felt comfortable. They had done this walk many, many times over the decades and centuries. He hadn't realized until just now how much he enjoyed it.

And missed, really missed her company.

The stars seemed to just fill every ounce of the sky, cutting out the dark shape of Florida Mountain to the west and War Eagle Mountain to the east like a cookie cutter cut out shapes from white dough on a black table.

The temperature had dropped from the high of the day, but it was still a warm night with very little breeze.

The climb soon winded both of them.

"Not used to this altitude," Bonnie said.

"How long were you working at the hotel before I got here?" Duster asked.

"Just a month. Came up here from San Francisco when I noticed some history going wrong. Small things, but enough to send me here."

"Amazing how two people can change so much in just a few short decades," Duster said, laughing.

"It never seems to fail, does it?" Bonnie said. "Luckily there are an unlimited number of timelines."

"Infinite number," Duster said.

"So how come the mine is killing people this time around? It's never done that before."

"Not that we know of," Duster said.

"Yeah, good point," Bonnie said. "But is someone in there running the deaths?"

"Infinite timelines," Duster said. "Remember? How could anyone from the future even find us?"

"Oh, yeah," she said.

"I just think it's the timeline trying to adjust is all. Spit us out in a manner of speaking."

She laughed. "Sometimes I do feel like something stuck in someone's tooth."

He laughed. "You always know how to kill a good metaphor."

"I've had a lot of practice," she said, also laughing. Her wonderful laugh carried over the barren mountainside and faded under the stars.

They walked the rest of the way in silence, both sweating slightly and panting from the climb.

At about eight hundred feet up the open face of the mountain above the mining town, they moved off the main wagon trail to the right and followed what was not much more than a trail up a gulley.

At one point a lot of Florida Mountain had been covered in different trees, but all of them were gone at this point in history, used in building the towns along the creek and stoking the ore mill fires.

Now they were walking along in scrub brush, following a trail that was left over from when the Trade Dollar had been a going concern. It had been closed down now for over forty years, the gold vein officially pinched off.

Actually, when they came back into a timeline, Duster always bought the mine and then willed it to his grandfather. This very afternoon he had sent the deed to Boise to be delivered to his grandfather in twenty years.

Duster always felt it was better to get the mine in control when he could and then lock it up.

"I'll never get used to the difference," Bonnie said, indicating the hillside around them.

"Me neither," Duster said.

In their original time in 2014, all the trees had grown back over this mountain, at least most of it. Silver City was only a ghost town with a few buildings left and a tourist trap in the summer. The Trade Dollar Mine was only a name on a map and a tailing pile covered in scrub brush.

Duster's father had taken him to the mine when Duster turned twenty-one and showed him what the mine was capable of doing.

Duster and Bonnie had been married at the time for only a year, and when they first started going back in time, they went as a couple, him working as a marshal, her the marshal's wife.

But after a dozen timelines and a few hundred or so of their own years, they decided to go their own ways. For the last ten timelines and two hundred plus years or more, they had gone in different directions.

Often they didn't see each other for decades, until the end of each timeline that is, when their very presence started to unbalance things.

And cause things like those poor men's deaths for no reason.

When Duster and Bonnie left, the timelines stabilized.

They finally reached the top of the old mine tailings. A small shack sat to one side of the tunnel entrance and small ore car rail tracks came out of the mine tunnel, went through the shack and to the end of the tailing pile.

Nothing looked disturbed as far as Duster could tell in the dark, even though neither of them had been up here in thirty years.

But he didn't feel the need to check. Besides, up here on the mountain he had no plan on shining a light on anything. A dozen people around the valley would see it and wonder and maybe investigate and that was the last thing they needed.

This mine just needed to sit abandoned until his grandfather came to investigate it and follow the instructions Duster had given him with the deed to get in.

Duster and Bonnie moved over to the mine entrance. It looked like it was solidly boarded up and in the starlight and faint moonlight nothing had bothered the old wood.

Duster took a skeleton key from the lining of his coat.

Bonnie had two of the very same thing and Duster had another sewn into his hat as well. They had also hidden a key a couple hundred yards from the mine just in case.

Duster pointed the skeleton key at the door and then turned the top head of the key.

There was a click and a slice of rock moved aside near the entrance. Duster moved over and put his palm print on the exposed panel.

Another click and what looked like a boarded-up mine entrance swung open. The wood was attached on the outside to a vault-like metal door that would withstand a lot of dynamite blasts.

Bonnie and Duster stepped inside and the door slid closed behind them, plunging them for a moment into blackness before the automatic light came up.

It still looked like an old mine tunnel inside at this point, even though Duster had reinforced the walls completely when they first came back to this timeline. The ore car tracks ran down the middle of the tunnel and lights strung along one side gave the tunnel a golden look.

"Good to be home," Duster said.

"I liked my place in San Francisco," Bonnie said.

Duster didn't say anything. This time around he hadn't settled down anywhere, but instead had just kept moving around, living in luxury hotels and being waited on. But even that had gotten old now that he thought about it.

They headed deeper into the mountain, the lights in front of them turning on as the lights behind them shut off.

The tunnel and the ore car tracks along the floor at one point turned right, but both Bonnie and Duster kept walking straight and through a wall that was nothing more than a hologram. Another level of protection in case someone got inside.

Beyond the hologram was a large chamber with tables and supplies stacked along the walls. Supplies they hadn't needed.

They just kept walking in silence into another small tunnel on the other side of the room and through another hologram that looked like the tunnel had dead-ended.

Beyond that was a large metal door that Duster unlocked and pushed open and then stepped through.

The lights came on and they were greeted with a sight very few people had ever seen.

They faced all of time.

The sight always took his breath away.

Seemingly every inch of the huge chamber walls were covered in crystals that reflected the light into a thousand colors over and over. The human mind couldn't really hold everything it saw in this room.

The chamber stretched slightly downward into the distance as far as anyone could see. The ceiling was a dome thirty feet over his head, the floor flat and dirt-covered. Every inch covered in those fantastic crystals.

His father had told Duster the chamber just kept on going and going and going since his grandfather had tried to hike it and gotten lost and never returned.

Duster had studied the physics of time and space at MIT for three years after his father had shown him this chamber the first time. Duster had come to figure that more than likely the chamber went through many dimensions of space and just expanded as it needed to.

The crystals looked like quartz crystals on first glance, only rose colored and multi-sized. They were of no mineral anyone had ever heard of and could not be removed from the walls. Some crystals were huge, others smaller than a tiny finger.

The amazing thing was that every crystal was an alternate timeline.

Every time anyone made a decision, a new crystal was formed for that timeline and that decision. If the decision was minor, the crystal stopped growing and was absorbed back into the larger crystal.

But when decisions had an impact down through time, then the crystal kept growing and millions and millions of new crystals were formed from it.

An infinite number of alternate universes, an infinite number of chambers stretching into infinite numbers of universes.

And every alternate timeline represented by a single crystal somewhere in this vast and unending cave.

It made Duster's mind hurt every time he thought about it.

In the middle of the room near the door was a long wooden table and on the table was a simple-looking machine. It drew power from the crystals when attached.

Duster often wondered in how many other timelines his father or someone else had discovered this room, built a machine like the one he and Bonnie had built.

More than likely millions or billions.

And he kept thinking someday he and Bonnie would meet up with themselves if they kept living like this long enough.

But with an infinite number of alternate timelines, the odds were so large, it would be hard to calculate.

Duster moved to the machine and then glanced at Bonnie. "You ready?"

"As always," she said, moving over and holding onto the edge of the machine near his hand. If they were touching the machine, they would keep the memories from that timeline.

He flipped the switch on the machine and then carefully unhooked the wire that led from the machine across the floor to a crystal about head-high on the wall. When they had hooked the machine up to that crystal, it had been a tiny side crystal off a larger one. Now it covered most of fifty feet of wall with hundreds of thousands and thousands of smaller crystals around it.

As they watched, many crystals were absorbed into the larger crystals as that alternate universe reset itself because of their absence.

Basically, that alternate universe had spit them out like a watermelon seed.

Duster glanced around at Bonnie. Even though she was still wearing the waitress uniform of the Dewey Hotel, it no longer fit her. She was back to her twenty-five-year-old body.

They were now back in 2014. In this time, this timeline, they hadn't been gone for more than a few minutes, even though he had clear memories of living for over thirty years in that other timeline.

He stared at Bonnie. She looked damned good, he had to admit that. He had missed her.

He still had on the duster and his hat, but it felt larger as well. He was also in his twenty-five-year-old body.

"You want to head home?" he asked, smiling at her. Home being their house in Boise in 2014. He could barely remember what it looked like, they had been gone so long. "Get caught up on what has happened to each other the last few decades?"

She smiled back, her eyes gleaming. "You know it's been almost three hundred years our time since we went home?"

"Really?" he asked, then realized she was right. No wonder he could barely remember their house and this modern world. The last five times they had just re-set, connected to a new alternate universe crystal and gone back. And each time had lasted over thirty years. Once they had actually made it long enough for their presence to not sink the Titanic in 1912.

"Really," she said, glancing at a watch she had left on the table. "We've aged here about five hours, but been gone almost three hundred years. Wild, huh?"

"Then we really have some catching up to do," he said, pulling off his duster and laying it across one end of the table, then taking off his hat and dropping it on the table as well.

She took off her apron and tossed it beside his coat and hat.

He offered her his arm. "Think you can remember how to drive after all the years?"

"Not a chance. That's up to you," she said, laughing. "I'm not trying to drive any new-fangled contraption off this hill.

But I do want to feel air-conditioning again."

"Oh, wouldn't that be nice," Duster said. "And the taste of a giant hamburger with pickles."

She laughed. "A shower. Just a simple shower instead of a bath. And real hot water not heated over an open fire."

Duster laughed, starting to remember all the things he had forgotten about while living in the past.

"That sounds heavenly," he said, "now that I think of it. We just have to come home more often. And maybe stay home a little longer," he said, squeezing her hand.

"I'd like that, Marshal," she said, laughing.

As they left the huge cavern that contained all of time, the automatic lights dimmed behind them.

On one wall to the left of the metal door a very small, very simple new crystal formed.

# Now Available
## from all your favorite booksellers
## in trade paper and electronic editions.

USA TODAY BESTSELLING AUTHOR

DEAN WESLEY

SMITH

AGAINST TIME

A SEEDERS UNIVERSE NOVEL

Dean Wesley Smith

*USA Today* Bestselling Writer

On Top
of the Dead

A Benny Slade Story

*Benny Slade came out of his vault one December afternoon to find the world changed.*

*Something instantly killed almost everyone in the city, including his two employees. The death stretched beyond the city. The event killed almost all the humans on the planet.*

*Benny has to figure out how to survive in a city full of dead bodies.*

*And maybe help build a new future for humanity.*

*A vastly altered version of this story was part of the Seeder's Universe novel* The High Edge.

# ON TOP OF THE DEAD

## ONE

Somehow I survived everyone else in the world dying.

One minute everyone was alive, the streets of New York were teeming with all sorts as is the case with this fine city; Then I went into my old steel vault at Benny Slade's Personal Loans to get some cash for my next loan, and when I come out, everyone was dead.

Car alarms were going off and the street in front of my place was a mess. Bodies littered the sidewalks, dead people filled wrecked cars, slumped over their steering wheels, or heads back, bodies held up by their seat belts.

And both Madge and Maggie, my two right hands, were both face down on my newly installed brown carpet.

Madge, who looked more like my old mother used to look before she got hit by that cab, had fallen next to her desk; while Maggie, about two years younger than my thirty-five years of age, had sprawled in the middle of the floor, her short skirt riding up and showing me a little of those wonderful white panties of hers that I liked so much.

I called out to Maggie and checked her first, then Madge. Both were dead. I sat back, feeling that cold, hard feeling come over me like it did when I had been in a firefight in the Gulf. Emotions got shoved back and I just stared.

It took me a minute to figure out what was different, what was wrong besides two healthy women being suddenly dead. There was no blood. Nothing. Now that I had turned them over, they just lay face up, eyes wide open, completely dead.

My first thought was gas attack, so I scrambled back into the vault; but I had left the vault door slightly open when I came out, so if it was some sort of terrorist gas attack, I was as good as dead as well.

After a minute sitting in the dark, I got disgusted at myself. "Come on, Benny, get it together," I said out loud. Madge had always complained I talked to myself too much, but Maggie thought it cute.

Maggie thought anything I did cute, and I thought she was cute, and we had flirted since the first day I hired her six months before. She was as sharp as they came and knew money and books and computers. I had somehow managed to keep the relationship on only flirt level.

I stared at Maggie for a moment. I was going to miss those white panties she flashed at me all day. I was going to miss her laugh and her smile and that wonderful blonde hair.

The coldness inside me whelmed upwards and I pushed those thoughts away. As my sergeant used to say, "Time to fight: time to think later if you survive the fight."

Clearly this was some sort of strange fight I was in.

I turned away from Maggie and headed for the door.

The moment I opened the door, the wave of sound hit me like a hammer. Hundreds and hundreds of car alarms were all going off at the same time.

Cars engines were still running, some racing as if their dead occupant still had a foot on the gas. Up Lexington Avenue I could see a fire starting to take hold of a building.

But what I didn't hear were police and ambulance sirens.

And no one around me in the cars or on the sidewalk was moving.

No one.

The day was a nice cold but comfortable December afternoon, some faint sun beating down on the buildings, so I didn't need any coat at the moment.

I checked a couple of young girls on the sidewalk to be sure they were dead. They were as gone as Madge and Maggie.

Then up the street I saw some movement as people came up out of the subway and sort of stopped and stared.

"So I'm not the only one," I said, feeling fantastically relieved.

I started toward the other people, then saw a couple of them panic and flee back down into the subway, followed by the others.

"Won't help," I shouted. But no one was going to hear anything I said over the noise of the car alarms and engines.

But they were doing exactly as I had done when I ran back into my old safe.

I glanced around at the buildings towering over the canyon of Lexington Ave. I couldn't see one window opening, or anyone even peeking out at all the noise.

And as far as I could see in both directions, everything was stopped and bodies covered the sidewalks.

I walked up to the corner of 54th and looked both directions. Same thing along the tree-lined street.

Everyone was dead, knocked down by some sort of giant killer in an instant. From what I could tell, not a one knew what hit them. None of them looked shocked or panicked or showing any fear at all. Just normal expressions on very dead people.

"What happened?" I said out loud, but the words barely made it to my own ears in the noise of alarms and running cars.

Who knew that the end of the world was going to be so damned loud?

# TWO

**"I NEED** to find out how far this spreads," I said into the noise of the running engines and car alarms.

I could feel the panic I had learned to hold down when I was a kid in fights on the street start to ease up into my gut. I hadn't felt that in many years. It wasn't the dead bodies that bothered me, I had seen worse in the Gulf. Much worse.

After the first few months in Iraq, dead bodies had stopped bothering me, at least on the surface. My counselor at the VA said I had a lot of buried anger and that the only way to get healthy was to let out some of the anger and tell him what I had seen. I didn't want to tell anyone, so

he and I hadn't gotten too far in the last few years.

Death didn't really scare me; but there were dead bodies on my street, in my own business, and I was still alive. Now that scared hell out of me.

I started to head back to lock up my safe, then laughed at myself and looked around. Unless this was the second coming and everyone was going to suddenly spring back to life, locking up my money was the least of my worries.

But I went in and locked the safe anyway, tossing the money back inside that I had taken out to loan Mrs. Tenny for her grandkid's operation. More than likely, Mrs. Tenny and her grandkid weren't going to be needing much of anything anymore.

Then I headed downtown along Lexington, stepping over and around the dead bodies on the sidewalks. I thought these sidewalks used to be crowded when people were alive. When the same people are sprawled all over the place, the sidewalks got even smaller.

Down a dozen blocks I saw a few more people gathered near the subway entrance, looking terrified and very panicked, but at least this group had gotten over the desire to flee back into the tunnels.

I crossed the street. "Anyone have any idea what happened?"

All four of them, including a nice-looking young thing with a backpack over her shoulder, shook their heads no.

One guy held up his cell phone. He looked to be about five years older than me and had more hair than any guy his age should ever have. "Phones are working, but no one is answering anything. Anywhere."

He stressed the word "anywhere."

He seemed to be the one who had taken charge of the little group. Besides the college-age girl, there were two boys about the same age, all looking stunned. More than likely this had been some sort of field trip for a class, and the older guy was the professor.

He stressed the word "anywhere" again, more than I wanted him to.

The other three nodded, all holding their cell phones as if they were lifelines. After walking a dozen blocks, I was starting to get the idea that no one was going to toss any of us a lifeline.

"Anyone try tuning in a radio?" I asked.

The guy nodded. "Nothing. The internet is still working, so is Facebook and Twitter, but not one new post from anyone anywhere in the world that we can tell. We are searching. And no one, including family across the country, is answering any of us."

"Are they all dead?" the young college-age girl asked, the look of panic in her eyes. I had seen that look a number of times in soldiers' eyes in Iraq. She was about to flip and I wanted no part of that.

"They might be," I said. "I'd head off the island, get away from the city."

The professor-guy nodded.

"We can't drive, and the subways aren't working," the girl said, her voice higher than a moment ago.

The guy who seemed in charge of his little group said softly, "Let's walk."

He turned them toward the river. "You coming?"

"Got to check on a few people first," I said.

"We'll head south if you want to join us."

"Thanks," I said to him. "I might."

I reached into my wallet and handed him my card. "Cell phone number. Call me if you hear anything or end up back this way—if the phones are still working."

I had no intention at that moment of joining anyone, but better to leave the options open. At least this group seemed to be holding together, except for the girl.

He nodded and tucked my card into his pocket. "Good luck," he said and followed his little flock.

I was starting to think the human race needed the luck now. No one online, no emergency declared, and no announcements coming across any emergency bands or over the radio. I had a hunch that no help was coming. That group could walk all the way to Florida and never find help other than other survivors.

I had a hunch that most of the human race had just bought the farm in a really big way.

Clearly being down in the subway had saved a number of people, and me being in my vault had saved me from whatever killed all these people. It hadn't been gas and it hadn't been an attack. That much was clear. I had read an article last week about some huge burst of energy that might take out the entire planet coming from some other sun. Maybe something like that had happened without warning.

Or maybe this had been an alien attack. That thought made me smile. I had clearly watched far too many late night movies. Maggie really liked those old bug-eyed monster movies. I had really liked when she sat on my couch watching television. It had been a fair trade.

I was never going to know the answer to the question of what happened, I was certain. And to be honest, I didn't much care. What I did care about was staying alive now that I had drawn the lucky straw.

I headed toward Broadway along 42nd Street, working my way among the bodies.

What was really creepy about the bodies was the lack of blood. All the bodies I had seen in the past had become dead bodies because of holes that let out a lot of blood. No one sprawled on the sidewalk around me now had anything more than a slight bloody nose from hitting their face when they fell.

And since it was December, they had all mostly been bundled up, so most of them looked like nothing more than piles of clothing with an arm or a couple legs sticking out.

I wandered all the way over to Broadway, seeing only a few survivors picking their way through the streets of dead. I turned and went up Broadway, then finally, a couple hours later as the sun was starting to set, I found myself back at my loan company on Lexington.

It had been a nice little business, funded by investors to help those on the streets who needed help to get by with short-term, interest-free loans. I had felt good running the little shop, helping out people, and Madge had been fantastic at getting us grants and donors to keep us going.

I went into my little business and pulled both Madge and Maggie out onto the sidewalk and sat them with their backs against the front of the business, like they were taking a break and just looking out over the street. I smoothed down Maggie's dress so her white panties didn't show.

I had been around enough dead bodies to know that after a while they would start smelling. No point in having Madge and Maggie smell up my office.

I stood on the sidewalk and looked in both directions, suddenly realizing something that was very obvious. This entire city was going to be one stinking mess in very short order. It was scheduled to freeze tonight, and that would help with the people outside, but everyone who had

died with the heat on in their apartments and businesses were going to start smelling really, really bad very shortly.

I had smelled my share of three-or-four-day-dead bodies and didn't much care for it.

I sat in my chair behind my desk, put my feet up, and tried to think while keeping the cold of the "emotion screen," as my counselor called it, in place. Breaking down now might just end up getting me as dead as everyone else.

Outside the car alarms had calmed down and the city was actually much quieter than I ever remembered hearing it, even late at night.

I looked around at the business I had put my heart into since getting out of the service, and sighed. "Not much to do here. I think you need to figure out what to do with the next part of your life, Benny. Right?"

No one answered me. My voice just echoed, and that seemed damn creepy as well.

I stood and headed back out into the light of the city, heading home. Luckily the electrical systems were still working, the stoplights still going through their cycles, the streetlights and building lights still making the night in the city seem like daylight.

More than likely that wouldn't last very long without people maintaining the power systems and lines. First good winter storm, and this place would be a giant frozen city of dead meat.

My apartment felt unusually silent, so I clicked on the television, hoping to find something or someone to tell me what happened.

Nothing. Some stations that had automatic programming were running, but the rest were just dead air.

The radio was the same, so I finally tuned the radio to an automatic light jazz station and let it play just to have some background music.

Then using my computer, another appliance that would soon be worthless, I pulled up some maps of New York and the area going south.

After an hour of studying those, I decided the idea was too stupid for words. Assuming I made the hike all the way to Florida, even taking some cars once I was outside of the city, what was I going to do down there with alligators and snakes and rotting-in-the-sun bodies?

"Think, Benny, think!"

I couldn't think of one darned thing, so I decided to make sure this was as bad as I had a hunch it was. I started dialing friends I knew in Southern California, Chicago, even Texas. I even dialed five of my old buddies who were still stationed overseas. Not a one answered.

I dialed twenty people. All machines or no answer. Not rock-solid proof things were bad everywhere, but adding in the internet and television silence, enough for me.

So I grabbed a yellow pad and asked myself, "What are you going to need to survive this winter?"

Then I started making a list.

—I was going to need power for lights and heat for long term.

—I was going to somehow need to figure out a way to get a place that I could hold back the smell until that passed, which was going to take some time and help from Mother Nature.

—I was going to need a place to store food and lots of canned supplies and safe drinking water.

—And considering the nut cases in this town that might still be alive, I was going to need a place I could protect.

—And from the faint glow out my window from the building on fire ten blocks up the street, I would need a place that wouldn't easily burn.

And maybe I could get a band of other survivors together who could work together to search for food and for defense.

Now I liked the sound of that.

I walked over to the window and stared toward the center of the city. Suddenly I could see it. The answer was right there in front of me. I knew exactly the place that fit the bill perfectly. But I was going to have to move fast, before anyone else had the same idea.

# THREE

**I COOKED** myself a good steak dinner and scanned the television and radio channels again as I ate, coming up blank yet again. Nothing was working besides automatic systems, and those weren't going to last long at all.

I put my coat on with my trusty .45 in one pocket and a flashlight in the other, and headed out.

At night, even with the lights of the city still completely on, the bodies looked even stranger, piled and sprawled on the sidewalk. It took me a good hour to reach the Empire State Building.

I figured the Empire State Building had pretty much everything I would need. It was a secured building so I could defend it. It would have a pretty fine security system and extra supply of weapons for the guards, and it would have generators. Lots of generators to run all those elevators during power failures. I think the building had something like eighty different elevators or something like that. Also it was high enough and windy enough that even at the worst of the smell, it should be survivable.

The biggest problem was going to be clearing out the bodies. I was going to need to do that quickly as soon as I made sure the building actually did have everything I needed.

By ten in the evening I had borrowed the keys off a guard's body and found the security room. It had a lot of cameras that all seemed to be working.

Nothing was moving on any of the cameras.

Nothing.

"Benny, you've got yourself into a real mess this time."

Staring at all the bodies showing on those cameras, I almost decided to just pack and head for Florida. Then I shook that thought away. This city was my home and I'd be damned if I was going to let the fact that most everyone was dead scare me off.

It took me another half hour in the security room to clear out the guards' bodies and then to find all the generators for all the floors and the ones that ran the elevator. They had more than enough fuel, and when that ran out I could re-supply easily.

And there was a good-sized water tank up high that had electrical pumps. I was going to have to check every room to make sure all the water was turned off so that didn't drain out when the power shut off.

The Empire State Building was all offices and meeting rooms and tourist stuff. No apartments, so I would have to find a really high office and clean that out and set myself up an apartment. That would be easy to do.

For the next hour I went around taking all the keys and guns from the guards and then locking the five main entrances to the building. That felt weird, like I was locking out the dead, but if I wanted to be secure, no point in taking any chances that some other survivors had this idea.

The last thing I needed was survivors with more guns than I had.

I went back to the main security area and spent the rest of the night making sure I knew all the details of the building, or at least as much as I could find. I didn't want to be on an elevator with no chance of rescue when the power went out. I needed to know that the backup generators would kick in, and if that didn't happen, how to do an emergency escape. I was going to be spending a lot of time in those elevators. Being trapped alive in one with no chance of rescue scared me cold.

# FOUR

**SOMEWHERE ALONG** the way, I fell asleep for a few hours on a cot in a side room off the security area.

An alarm woke me up.

I scrambled to the screens, at first not remembering where I was or what had happened. Then I saw all the bodies and nothing moving.

An alarm was flashing that it was time to open the doors.

I shut it off, dropping the room back into silence.

A radio in the back gave me no more hope than it had yesterday.

Outside it looked cold and overcast. That was good for the moment, since it would slow down the decay on the people in the streets.

I banged open a candy machine in the break room and feasted on a breakfast of a couple packs of nuts and a Diet Coke.

From what I could tell from the ever-changing monitors, there had to have been thousands of people in this building when humanity's number came up. No way I was going to be able to move all of them before they would start smelling.

I was just going to have to go up high, to the 102nd-floor observatory, and work my way down, clearing every body I could find from as many of the top floors as I could.

About a third of the way up, you have to change elevators, and there were a lot of bodies in that area, so I just figured a few more there wouldn't hurt.

But when I got to that lobby, I decided that was a bad idea. I was going to have to go through that transition floor all the time. I needed to clear that first.

I went down three floors, then using a large fire ax, I broke out some of the windows in an office there, letting in the cold wind from outside.

First I dragged all the bodies in that large office area to the window and just dumped them out. After about thirty bodies, a couple of which could have used less pasta when alive, I decided I was going to need a better system.

I had no doubt that some of the protections built into the side of the Empire State building to catch falling bodies would stop some of the ones I'd tossed, but after about twenty, the bodies would make it all the way to the street below.

I got a large cart from the shipping and receiving area and went all the way to the top. It took me two hours to clear off the two-dozen people on the top observation deck and take them down a dozen floors to another empty office suite, where I again broke out a window. Only this time I just stacked the poor souls near the window to take care of later.

By eleven in the morning I knew that stacking those bodies there wouldn't help my situation at all. I had to toss them outside. Which meant that by the time I got done clearing out the bodies in this building, there would be a stack of human flesh a story tall around north base. I would be living on a pile of the dead.

I was moving like a zombie, and considering what I was doing, that seemed about right. Like we used to say in the service, I was walking dead. Not a way to keep from making a mistake and getting injured or killed. I was going to need more food and more rest, if that was possible.

I went back down to the security area and did a check of the area outside the building.

Nothing but death.

I ate a quick lunch of some guard's sandwich stored in the fridge and then took another nap. Two hours later I was just about ready to go again when my cell phone rang in my pocket and scared hell out of me.

"Yeah," I said.

"This is the man you met yesterday with the three college kids," the voice on the other end said.

"Find anything?" I asked, for a moment excited at the idea that I might be wrong about everyone being dead.

"Nothing," the man said. "We're coming back to the city. It's where we all live, doesn't seem right leaving it. You got any ideas on where to hole up to get through the winter?"

My stomach twisted in disappointment, then pushed that aside as I had been pushing all feeling aside since this started.

I glanced at the security cameras showing room after room of bodies and shrugged. Why not? I could use the help.

"I'm setting up in the Empire State Building," I said. "It won't burn, it's got generators, a great security system, and a good water supply. It can be defended."

"And it's high enough to escape some of the smell," the guy said.

I was impressed. He had been worrying about the same thing.

"You and your merry band want to join me?" I asked. "There's a lot of work to do."

"It will take us about three hours to get there," he said. "Thanks."

"Pick up anyone else you see that looks sane along the way," I said. "This is one big building. Go to the South Entrance. I'll be waiting there in three hours."

"Okay," the professor said.

"And one more thing. Stay away from the north side of the building."

"Why?" he asked, then before I could tell him he said, "Oh, I understand."

This guy really was smart. That was good. It was going to take my street smarts and military training and his brains to keep any of us alive through the winter.

"Three hours; call me if you get stuck or run into problems."

"Three hours," he said and hung up.

I once again checked the television and radio. Nothing.

At least I was going to have help.

# FIVE

**I TOOK** some lumber from the maintenance area and went back up to the floor where I had broken out the window. There I spent an hour building a ramp for the shipping cart that slanted slowly up to the broken window.

Then I went back to the floor under the top observation platform and worked my way down, room-by-room, office-by-office, floor-by-floor, using the cart to take the bodies I found to the ramp and dumping them out the window. Luckily for me, some of those floors were empty, thanks to the recession.

Or a slow day at the office.

In one office, it made me sad when I found twenty very attractive women. I would have dated any of them. And that thought made me miss Maggie.

I even missed Madge.

I just hoped that some women had survived besides that panicked college girl. With luck, we would build a nice little community right here in the Empire State building.

With luck.

I found a nice hide-a-bed couch in one executive's office on the seventy-ninth floor, and decided that's where I would bunk for the night later. The office also had a really nice bathroom and shower, and I was really needing a shower.

Exhausted, I went downstairs to the south entrance at three hours, making sure my .45 was still tucked in my pocket.

No sign of the professor and his class; so I went across the street to a deli and got some great roast beef from the fridge and made myself a sandwich. I was really going to miss fresh meat.

I got enough food for three meals tomorrow and went back across the street.

There were three bodies in the deli, and another near the door, but I just didn't have the energy to do anything with them at the moment. But I would have to, since that deli had a back room full of supplies and some nice freezers full of meat. If I could get a couple of those freezers across the street and hooked up to a generator, maybe I'd have meat for the winter.

I was back inside the lobby of the Empire State Building, and was about to lock the door, when I saw the professor and his three charges winding their way along the sidewalk.

They all looked tired and clearly depressed, and the girl had lost her backpack along the way.

I propped the door open and waited for them, chewing on the sandwich.

"Thanks, Benny," the professor said, extending his hand. "My name is Professor C.M. Green." He laughed. "Not sure what I'm a professor of anymore."

He had managed to pull back his long hair and tie it, and I could tell he had been a gym rat. He was strong, of that I had no doubt. He had a firm grip, but I could tell that the last day had really worn on him. I'm sure I looked just as bad to him.

He quickly introduced me to the two college boys. The redhead with bright freckles who stood about six foot high, was called David. The other kid, shorter with a lot of pimples, was Freddy. Both looked like they could use some muscle and about fifty pounds. The girl was named Constance. She had long brown hair, long fingernails, and the remains of some makeup on her brown eyes. She looked like she was about to pass out.

"You had any food?" I asked them.

The professor shook his head. "Just snacks is all."

"So that's job one," I said.

I had them leave their stuff just inside the building entrance, tossed the professor a group of keys from a guard, locked up the building, then headed across the street to the deli.

"Boys," I said, "can you clear out those bodies and move them a little ways down the sidewalk while the professor and I fix you something to eat?"

Both boys looked horrified that they would have to touch a dead body, and the professor didn't look too pleased himself.

"Do it this way," I said, grabbing the man's body near the door by both feet right at the ankle. Then I just dragged him away from the door and down the sidewalk. "Don't try to pick them up, and if you don't want to use your bare hands, there's a store two doors down that has leather gloves. Bring me and the professor back two pair of larges each as well."

I stopped dragging the body, then led the professor and the girl into the deli as the two boys went for gloves.

"There's a lot of work to get that building ready," I said as the professor and I went in behind the counter.

"I can't even imagine," he said.

"You won't have to imagine," I said. "You're going to get to see it for yourself as soon as we're done eating."

The boys cleared the bodies out of the deli and then we all sat and ate sandwiches with soda. It almost seemed normal. The professor told me how far they had walked before turning back. They had stayed the night in a furniture store, but most of them hadn't slept much.

All of them had families they were convinced were dead, and the professor had a wife. "We're all going to need to find our families and check on them," he said. "It's why we came back."

My only family had been Madge and Maggie. Both my parents had died in a boating accident while I was in Iraq. I knew Maggie and Madge were dead. I would have looked for them as well if I hadn't known. Especially Maggie.

"I can understand that," I said.

He nodded thanks.

"Any idea at all what caused this?" I asked as the conversation lagged.

"Quasar pulse," Freddy said.

"Aliens," David said.

The professor shook his head. "All kinds of theories; no facts."

I nodded. "Well, back to the task of survival then. We need to get as much of the building cleared and set up before things turn really sour."

"You mean everything smells?" the girl asked.

"It will. Worse than you can imagine," I said. "We'll work some more tonight, and then you all need some rest. How about tomorrow you take a student and go out one at a time to find that person's family? And maybe look for more sane people to join us. The rest of us will keep working."

"That's a really good plan," the professor said, trying and failing to sound upbeat. "Everyone up for that?"

They all just nodded and kept eating. If nothing else, this was the most well-behaved and smallest class I had ever seen.

After dinner, I first took them up to the security room and made sure they all knew the same things I did about the emergency generators and how to escape if they were stuck in an elevator when the power went out.

Then, pulling the professor aside, I suggested that the two boys start working on clearing out the main lobbies downstairs, dragging the bodies away from the main doors, that sort of thing. I then suggested that he and Constance start on the floor where I'd left off and check every bathroom in every office to make sure the water was turned off in every bathroom and lunchroom. Even the public ones in the lobbies.

"What are you going to do?" he asked, after he sent the two boys off with their assignments and instructions to call him on his cell if they needed him.

"I am going to keep working my way down, floor-by-floor, clearing bodies."

All three of us went all the way back to the top, double-checking to make sure I hadn't missed anyone in a maintenance area or in a back office, and that all the water was turned off. We worked our way down by taking the stairs.

I showed the professor and Constance my cart set-up and ramp when we reached that floor, then they went off checking the water and I kept working my way down, one body, one floor at a time. By the time two hours had gone by and it was dark, I had the top thirty floors completely cleared of bodies.

I had scouted the neighborhood a little, mostly with the exterior security cameras, and I knew there was another restaurant nearby, so we all headed there to scrounge for food, then a couple stores down to find bedding and to a neighboring store to find changes of clothes.

We cleared the bodies out of both places in only minutes, since we were going to need to use both places in the future.

I was starting to feel better by the minute.

It had only been a little over a day since the world ended and I had a hunch this new way of living just might work. We might actually have a way to survive, with enough help.

And a little more time.

# SIX

**WE GOT** the time.

For the next five days we tried to prepare the big building as much as we could. After dumping a few hundred bodies through windows, you started to get numb to what you were doing. And after the first few days, we were wearing masks and tossing our clothes out after working and taking long hot showers to try to clear the smell from our noses.

But we finally got every body we could find out of the big building.

The city was starting to smell as well, mostly from the bodies inside the other buildings. So after clearing the bodies from the entire building, our focus turned completely to stocking up on bedding, food, clothing, and just about anything else we thought we might need and could get on carts or carry.

I took the top office floor and the professor and his kids stocked up the twenty-second floor, since there were six bathrooms and lots of offices that could be made into bedrooms.

I wanted us to be prepared for a hundred people living in the building instead of just five, even though we hadn't seen anyone else since the first day. And the professor agreed. So we stocked food and blankets and propane heaters and lighting and everything else on a dozen different floors.

"The moment the lights go out in the city and lights are on in this building, people from all over will see us. We need to be ready."

All the kids had found their families, all dead. And every so often I would run across one of them crying. Nothing I could say to cheer them up. They were either going to make it or they weren't.

My counselor had taught me that. I had decided after that session that I would be one of the soldiers that made it. And I would make it this time as well.

Constance just slowly withdrew, working and eating less and less, no matter what any of us said. On the fifth morning she vanished, going out the south door before any of us got up. I had no doubt she wouldn't be back, but the professor wanted to go in search of her.

He took two gas masks we had gotten for long trips outside into the smell and he and Freddy went looking for her without luck.

As he and David were about to go out on a third search party trip, I stopped him. "It's safe out there. She knows where we are. If she wants to come back, she will."

We both knew by that point she never would.

# SEVEN

**THE POWER** cut out on the tenth day.

We all went to using propane lanterns and climbing stairs. The smell outside was getting so bad, none of us wanted to go out there.

I had set up a portable generator on a balcony outside of an office suite that I had converted to a very large apartment, with a big screen television and a movie library that would take me ten years to watch if I never stopped.

I had all the staircases boarded and sealed on my floor except for one, and that one I had fitted with steel bars locking it at night. And I had enough firepower to hold off a pretty good-sized attack. Not that I thought one was coming. I actually doubted it was, but in the Gulf I had seen my share of the underside of humanity. I had survived this, which meant scum might have as well. Not everyone was going to be nice guys like the professor and his kids.

When the power went out we made sure all the doors were locked again, then set up a twenty-four-hour guard system in the security room and kept the exterior and lobby camera systems running on generators. If anyone wanted in, we would see them.

It was on the twelfth day after humanity had been destroyed that the aliens showed up.

The day had broken clear and crisp, one of those wonderful New York winter days that made you want to go outside. And I would have, except for the smell.

The alien ships seemed to settle over the entire city, their massive shadows cutting off the sun completely. A couple of the ships had to be almost as big as the entire island and just hovered overhead.

The damn kid had been right. Aliens had wiped out humanity.

I called the professor on the walkie-talkies we had set up, and twenty minutes later he and the boys joined me in my apartment, staring out the large window at the alien ship closest to us.

I wouldn't even begin to try to describe it. Dark black with lots of different elevations on the bottom, like a city in and of itself was stuck to the bottom of the ship.

"They are here to rescue us," David said.

I glanced at David who was smiling. "Why would you say that?"

He kept his eyes on the huge ship. "They've been taking our kind to another planet for centuries. They knew we would be destroyed. They planned for it."

"And you know all this how?"

"He doesn't," Freddy said. "Since they are here it's pretty clear they were the ones that wiped us out like stepping on an ant hill. They just missed a few of us."

I was about to ask the kid why he thought that when a blue beam shot down from the ship and hit somewhere in the city. I was expecting noise or flash or smoke, but nothing.

"Now what are they doing?" I asked the two boys.

One said, "Rescuing."

The other said, "Killing."

The professor said nothing.

Then more and more beams slashed down on the city. But again that didn't seem to be like any weapon I had ever seen before. No smoke, no destruction.

Then a blue beam hit the professor and he vanished.

A moment later the two boys were gone.

Then suddenly there was a blue light around me, and the city and my office apartment and the alien spaceship vanished.

# EIGHT

**DAMN,** I wish I could say that was the end of it, that the kid who thought the blue beam was a weapon had been right. But, of course, it wasn't.

The blue beam was some sort of transportation device right out of Star Trek, only without the stupid music and sound effects.

I found myself standing beside the professor and the two boys, along with hundreds of other very tired and scared-looking humans who had survived the destruction of the world, only to be kidnapped by aliens.

"Perfect," I said. "Are we in the frying pan or in the fire?"

"I'm guessing fire," the professor said.

"We're lunch," Freddy said.

"I doubt they have a cookbook," David said.

I had no idea what they were talking about, but it didn't sound good that the aliens with the blue beam could want to eat humans.

Then one of the doors on one side of the room slid back, and one of the aliens walked into the room. Only it wasn't an alien. The guy looked as human as I do, only he was clearly more rested and clean in his white shirt and dark slacks and military hat.

The two or three hundred of us in the room just stared as he jumped up on a low stage. You could have heard the old pin drop in that room.

"Fine people of the great city of New York," he said. "Very sorry to startle you like this, but the next wave of the pulsar will be hitting Earth in just under four hours. We have over a hundred ships circling the planet, pulling all survivors from the first wave to safety."

"How come you couldn't get here before the first wave?" one guy shouted.

"And who are you, anyway?" someone else shouted.

The officer just smiled. "Let's just say I'm as human as the rest of you, and from a very distant place. We could not save everyone from the first wave, although we have saved millions over the centuries and humanity is flourishing just fine on five other planets around other stars. But we can save all of you who survived and let the second and final wave pass with no more deaths, and then put you back on Earth to rebuild."

"What happens if we don't want to go back to that graveyard?" one woman shouted.

A lot of people shouted "Yeah, what happens?"

Again the officer smiled and said, "We'll deal with that problem when the time comes. But for now, there is food and drink against the far wall and cots to take naps. This entire process will take about ten hours. Please relax, and I will be back to talk with you as soon as I can."

"One last question," the professor beside me shouted at the officer. "How many survived the first wave?"

"Worldwide," the officer said, smiling, "almost two million. And we'll get them all, I promise."

As the noise of three hundred people talking at once filled the room like a hard wave, I turned to David who had been talking about the aliens.

"Well, now what?"

"I have no idea," he said.

At that moment, a girl's voice called out, "Professor," and Constance hit the professor with a hug, sobbing.

Even I was glad to see she was still alive, but not as much as the boys in her class. She looked like she had gone through hell, and she smelled awful, like she had been sitting next to a dead body for days.

"Where have you been?" he asked, clearly fantastically glad to see her,

"At my mom's apartment," she said between sobs. "I hid when you came there looking for me."

That made sense. She had simply gone home to die beside her mother.

The owners of this big ship clearly were going to make sure that didn't happen. At least not for the next ten hours.

# NINE

**I HAD NO IDEA** how the hundreds of other people in the room felt, but I kept verging on sheer panic that came close to cutting through the black screen in my head and then five minutes later I would be elated to be a survivor.

After we had stood in line for some of the best-tasting food I had ever had, I asked the professor why he had asked the question about how many survivors.

"Because there is a magic number of humans that it takes to build a population and to survive and have a large enough gene pool to make the effort even worthwhile."

"And you know this how?"

"It's my field," he said, smiling. "Or it used to be."

"Is two million enough?"

He laughed. "Far, far more than enough."

At least that was good to hear.

During the next six hours, both the professor and I mentioned to numbers of people that we had set up the Empire State Building for survival, and if we were put back, they were welcome to join us. He and I had talked days before about how it would be an advantage to have a few hundred people in the building, all working toward the same goal of survival.

At nine hours, true to his word, the officer of the big spaceship came back in and everyone got quiet.

"Everyone has survived the second and final wave of deadly electromagnetic waves. We are returning to Earth and will be in orbit in about fifteen minutes."

"So do we have an option of going to another planet?" someone shouted.

"No," the officer said, which caused my heart to sink and the room to explode in shouting. I loved New York, but not in the condition it was right now. Anywhere would be better than that killing field.

The officer held up his hand for silence and got it. "We will take the wounded and the sick, but all of you, and the two million others on this ship and the other ships, are the future of humanity on Earth. We can't rob Earth of that."

"How do we survive?" someone shouted from behind where I stood, staring at the man in the white uniform who was sealing my fate.

"Some of you won't," he said bluntly. "But many will; enough to rebuild a wonderful culture and society and preserve much of what is already there. Your job is to save the old art and culture and build new on top of it."

Building on the dead was all I could think of, just as every society did.

Suddenly, beside the Professor, Freddy shouted out, "We won't remember any of this, will we?"

The officer smiled. "A few of you will," he said. "Most of you won't. And the ones that do remember won't be believed by the others."

That stunned everyone even more than the death sentence he had just declared on many people in the room.

"I wish each and every one of you luck," he said. "The future of the human race on the planet Earth depends on all of you."

With that, a wave of purple beams swept over the room and I knew I was going home, to the city I loved, and my new home near the top of the Empire State Building.

# TEN

**I AWOKE** with a slight headache on the carpet of my new office suite apartment. The professor and the two boys were sprawled on the carpet beside me.

The aliens had sent us all back to the exact spot we had been when taken.

"Aliens!" I said, jumping to my feet and looking out the window. The night sky looked bright, with many stars. Below most of the city was dark. No sign of any spaceship or anything odd.

Except for the fact that the professor and the two boys were passed out on the carpet behind me.

Crap, I was one of the people who would remember. Damn, that was all I needed inside my screwed up head. Had I imagined it all?

The professor moaned and sat up, holding his head. "What happened? How did I get up here?"

Beside him the boys were starting to stir.

I was about to tell him about the aliens, then decided against it. "What do you remember?"

"Nothing," he said.

"Boys," I said, "do you remember how you got up here?"

"No," both said at almost the same time, looking around.

"I think a milder version of what killed everyone hit us and knocked us out. I don't remember anything either."

"Maybe the aliens came," Freddy said.

Dave and the professor both just shook their heads.

"We'll figure out what happened tomorrow," I said. "We need to go hunt for Constance in the morning. I woke up with

an idea of where she might be. And I also have a hunch we're going to have some new tenants in the building soon."

"Bad dream?" the professor asked. "I didn't dream anything." He glanced at his watch. "We were out for a good twelve hours."

"Yeah," both boys said. "I doubt I could get any sleep."

I nodded in agreement. I had no doubt I could sleep. We had a very large world to rebuild, one person at a time.

"All right then," I said. "We need to go save Constance right now. Boys, you guard the security system, professor, get your gas mask on. You and I will go to her mother's apartment. I'm sure she's there."

"I always wondered about that," the professor said, shaking his head. "But we checked there."

"I think she was hiding from you the first time," I said.

Moving slowly toward the stairs with the boys following him, the professor said, "I sure wish I knew what happened."

"Aliens," Freddy said.

"A second weaker pulsar blast," David said.

I didn't want to try to tell them that they were both partially right. I wasn't sure if I believed it myself.

"We'll figure it out," I said. "Eventually. But right now my gut is telling me Constance needs our help. We do that first."

All three nodded and started down the stairs ahead of me.

I had once asked my counselor at the VA how he did his job every day, digging in the trash of people's minds trying to save them.

He just smiled and said, "I just do it one person at a time."

I had followed that motto when I opened my little loan office to help people, one person at a time. Now we had to dig around in the junk of a ruined planet and give a helping hand up to one person at a time.

And by doing that, given time, we just might build something a lot bigger.

—

 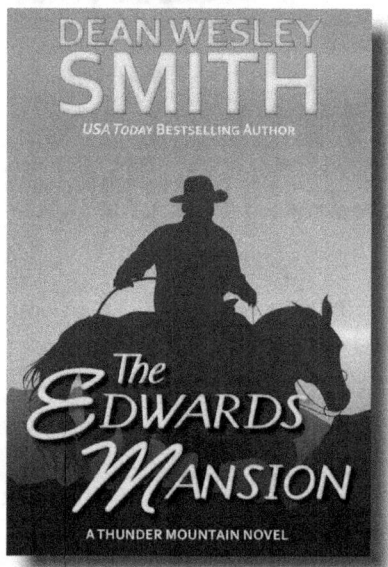

# Now Available
## from all your favorite booksellers
## in trade paper and electronic editions.

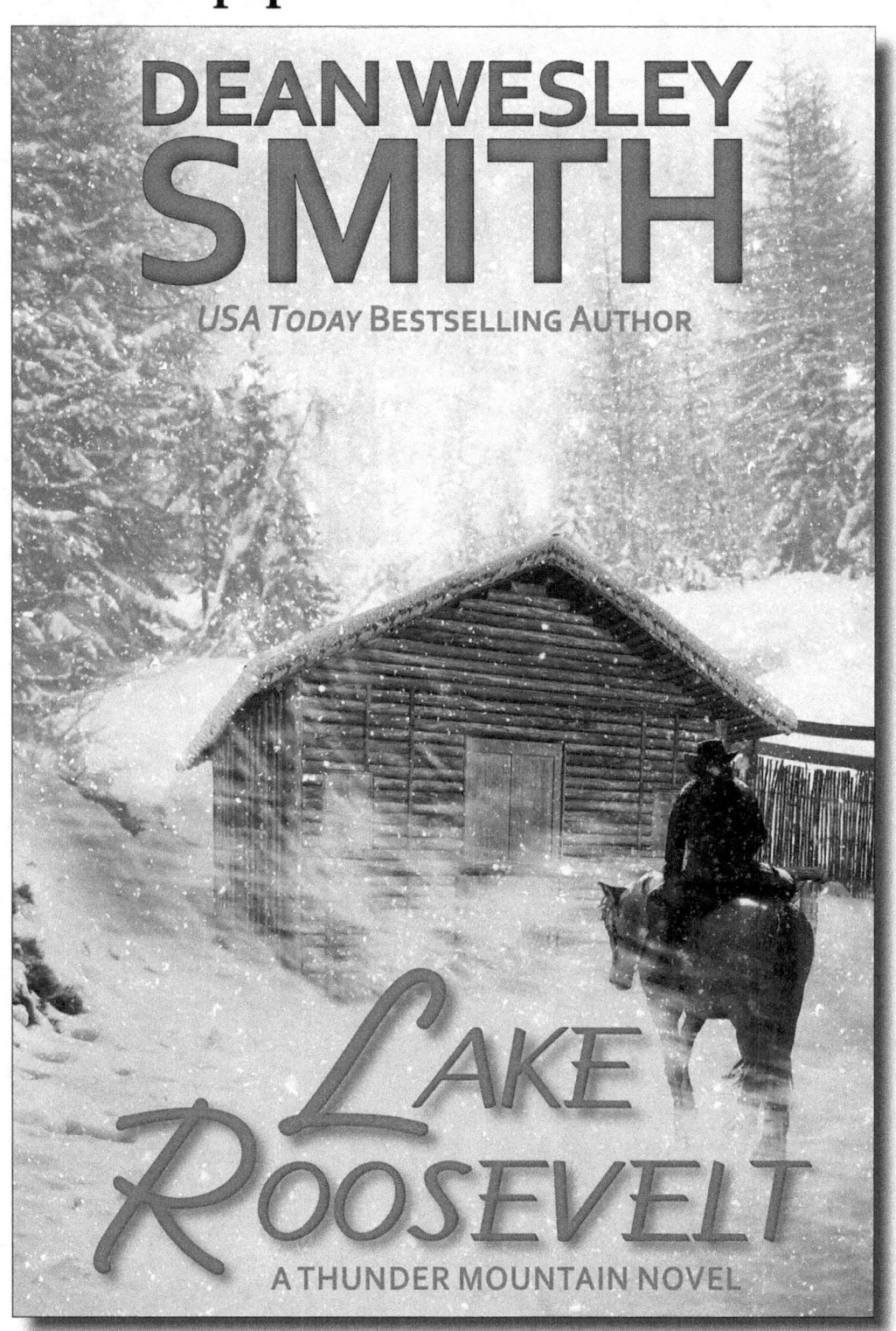

Dean Wesley Smith

*USA Today* Bestselling Writer

A Funny Look
at Love, Death,
and the Movies

THE YELLOW OF THE
FLICKERING PAST

*He killed her with a magic spell, buried her in the basement, and now she nags him every day to take her to the movies.*

*Just as she nagged him when she lived.*

*The woman never got tired of buttered popcorn and a dark theater.*

*A really strange ghost story about love, death, and the movies.*

*"The Yellow of the Flickering Past" was first published in the Daw Books anthology* Wizard Fantastic *edited by Martin H. Greenberg.*

# THE YELLOW OF THE FLICKERING PAST

## Act One:
## A Yellow Oil Mess

**SIXTEEN DAYS** after I killed her, I took my dead wife to a movie.

She had always loved movies.

Actually I think she loved the memory of movies more than any one film. And she loved the smell of the buttered popcorn you could buy in theaters, even if the butter was actually only a melted yellow oil from big yellow cans. She said it was part of the movie- going experience and that was all that mattered.

On our first date to a movie I laughed when she asked for an "extra large, extra butter, please."

"You know that shit will kill you?" I said as the guy with a thousand pimples pumped the handle of the butter machine like he was huddled over his first Playboy centerfold. Miss July.

"Sure," my date, soon-to-be wife, later-to-be-dead wife, had said. She never once offered me any of her popcorn. That was sort of how we argued from then on.

And we argued a lot.

She asked for the same "Extra large, extra butter" every time we went to a movie. She never missed a movie.

We went to a lot of movies.

Of course, people who saw us at the movies thought we made the perfect couple. "Fit together," they would say, but after I came out of the coma induced by new love and the first year of marriage, I just didn't see why. She was a light blonde, with a large, white-toothed smile, and wide, innocent green eyes. I actually had light brown hair, but I suppose it looked closer to her color because I kept it cut so short. I had dark brown eyes and people said I squinted a lot. I was almost five-six when I wore my good shoes, and even in heels she still wasn't as tall as I was.

Besides that, we argued all the time and I hated movies and didn't eat popcorn, especially with yellow oil.

The last year of our marriage I started daydreaming about the dreaded yellow oil. I figured no human body could digest that stuff, so it must have been building up in her body over the five years and seven days we were together. Maybe even for years before, just waiting for the right circumstances to set it all off in a huge bang. I dreamed she would explode and the police would just nod and say, "Yup. Yellow oil build-up."

But I could never figure out how to set off the explosion. I watched the papers for months hoping to read about another yellow oil explosion, but never did.

I even consented to sex one night that last year, thinking that might set her off.

But the thought of her exploding had me so excited that she said I didn't last long enough to even get her hot. Maybe that was why it didn't work.

Sadly, she never did explode, or even melt. The yellow oil didn't kill her.

I did that. I killed her with a curse from a book of Wizard curses I bought at a used bookstore downtown. A big brown book with a guy on the cover wearing a pointed hat and a star-covered robe.

I wish the yellow oil had killed her instead, in a huge, messy wife-explosion. I wouldn't have minded cleaning up the mess.

After my now-dead wife would get her "extra large, extra butter," she used to love the walk down the carpeted halls of the multiplex theater, past the posters of the other movies showing in all the other theaters. She would stop and point out every show she wanted to see, as if I really cared. The last few years I even stopped pretending I did care, but she kept right on pointing them out.

Then, after the pointing-at-the-poster routine was done she would go into the theater and look around in the low light to find just the right, perfect seat. Finding the exact right seat was always treated as one of the most important events in life. I think a good seat meant more to her than Christmas or her mother's birthday.

Once she had found that perfect place, she always whispered to me that she hoped no one would sit in front of her.

I always just nodded and she would settle in, happy, content, wide eyes focused on the blank screen ahead.

On the times when someone did have the nerve to take the seat in front of her, she would make a rude, almost pig-like noise and make us move to new, perfect seats. Which, of course, again took time.

And once settled she would again whisper to me that she hoped no one would sit in front of her.

For a popular movie we moved a lot and usually ended up sitting down front. Then I would get a sore neck from looking straight up at the screen. I always felt I was looking up the actor's nose. Nose hair can really distract from the plot of a movie.

I think, more than even the movie, I think my now-dead wife loved the previews of the coming attractions. Something about the possibility of a future trip to the movies held her spellbound like a deer in front of a car's headlights. We never saw a preview of a movie after which she didn't whisper to me that she wanted to see the movie. And didn't it look just wonderful?

The word "wonderful" was always followed by a long sigh. Just once I wish she would have sighed like that after we had sex.

Near the end of the second year of our marriage I started writing letters to the theater begging them, at first, and then demanding, that they not show previews of coming movies. A nasty phone call from the police department made me stop writing.

The theater kept playing the coming attractions.

She kept wanting to see every movie.

Of course, we went to them all.

And they all had coming attractions.

I still get dizzy just thinking about it.

That, and all that yellow oil she ate.

## ACT TWO: THE UNLAWFUL CHRISTMAS ARGUMENT

**THE IDEA** to take my dead wife to a movie was hers, of course. It seemed that my killing her, then wrapping her body

in plastic and stuffing it in an old trunk in the basement didn't even slow down her love for movies. I guess I was wrong to expect that it would.

For over two weeks after I killed her I kept saying no. No way in hell was I going to be seen in a movie theater with the ghost of my dead wife. And there were no curses or formulas in my Wizard's book for getting rid of ghosts, so I had to keep listening to her and arguing with her.

And of course, as when we were married, she ended up winning all the arguments. She finally used the old "it's-almost-Christmas" routine and I caved in like a tunnel cut through mud. But I said I would do it on my conditions.

She didn't care about that. But she did say we had to follow the ghost rules. Wizard curses, ghost rules, my conditions. This was going to be a very complicated trip to the movies.

Before I bought the Wizard's book, I didn't know Wizards even existed. And I never expected that I might be one, but since one of the Wizard curses worked for me, I suppose I am. But so far I've not been able to make another curse work. But I'm going to keep practicing, because what Wizards can do is really cool stuff.

Before she died I didn't realize that ghosts had rules, either. But they do. A lot of them. And I discovered the ghost rules are sometimes a little tricky to figure out. For example, there was the main rule about why she was still even around. She said she had her reasons and they were for her to know and me to find out. She said that a lot during our marriage and I never found out a thing.

I didn't expect that now that she was a ghost this time was going to be any different.

As far as going to a movie went, she figured that if I could get her body close enough to the theater, she, her ghost, not her body, could go inside with me and see the movie. For some ghost rule or another she had to stay fairly close to her body, which is why she had been hanging around the house.

She decided I could put her body in the car and then park the car next to the theater. A simple plan, really. Just get a two-plus week-old dead body right up next to a public theater and then leave it for two hours. I laughed at her when she said that was what we needed to do. I flat out said no way.

She kept at me, kept me up all night again with the what-a-wonderful-Christmas-present it would be for her. I tried a Wizard curse on her that was supposed to have turned her into a frog, but she stayed a ghost and kept at me.

I gave in again. About sunrise. Using Christmas in arguments should be outlawed in all marriages, even after death.

We waited until after dark, which really didn't upset her because she hated the cheap, early shows. She always said going to a regular show was much better. I never did figure out what was the difference between a cheap show and a regular show, except the price. Every time I asked her about the difference she just looked at me as if I was stupid and just couldn't see.

At least this time I would only have to buy one ticket.

As I loaded her body into the hatchback, she stood in the driveway to watch for the neighbors and cars on the street. It had only been a few weeks since she had died and the decay and smell wasn't too bad. Or at least I tried to convince myself that it wasn't that bad.

I had her wrapped in three sheets of plastic and taped so tightly shut no air, or anything else for that matter, could get in there. Yet I was sure as I draped her over my shoulder that I could smell a rotten, nose-clogging aroma of decay. Like a dead dog three days beside the road.

She laughed when I mentioned it and told me it was my guilt catching up with me. But I swore I could smell her rotting, right through the plastic bags and all the tape, guilt or no guilt.

It took what seemed like an eternity to get her body settled and the hatch closed. The backs of newer cars just weren't made for holding bodies like the trunks of the cars my parents owned. Those trunks were big. To get her in the Impala hatchback I had to remove the spare. No telling what problems we would have if we had a flat.

She came through the door without opening it and settled into the passenger seat.

"This is going to be so much fun," she said, and I shuddered. She had said those very words before every movie we ever went to, almost like a recording.

Maybe this was my hell. No maybe about it. I was in hell. I was destined to take my dead wife to a movie three times a week for the rest of my life. Maybe I should just kill myself now and get it over with.

If I could only be certain that would end it.

## ACT THREE:
## A YELLOW TINGE

**"YOU WON'T** think it's sweet if we get caught," I said about halfway to the theater after she told me I was being sweet for taking her to a movie. "I get tossed in jail for killing you, and you'll end up haunting the local cemetery."

She shrugged. "Couldn't be much worse than hanging around here with you."

"Now don't start," I said. "This is how you got killed in the first place.

"Don't you dare blame me again for what happened." She had her hands on her hips, the sign she was getting mad. "I'm the one who is dead, remember."

"How can I ever forget?"

Actually, I had never really totally hated her. At least not enough yet to kill her. But I suppose it was building to that. I sure had wished she was dead enough times.

It was her way of arguing that got to me. One afternoon she started in on me. Or, as she tells it, I started in on her. Either way doesn't make much difference. I got so mad I yelled a Wizard curse at her that I had just read that morning. She laughed, so for a special effect I tossed a handful of sparkle dust from the magic shop in her face. I read that Wizards were always using sparkle dust and I guess it worked.

She backed up away from me rubbing her eyes, tripped, and hit her head hard on the edge of the counter as she went down.

I was over her immediately. I didn't like the way her head hitting that counter had sounded. A sick, deep smacking and cracking sound. Granted, I had cursed her dead, but I wasn't sure I really wanted her that way.

Too late. She was already dead. And her ghost was standing above me leaning over her own body.

"Now see what you have done," she had said. Even dead she had started out annoying.

We rode the rest of the way in silence to the theater. I remembered we had done that a lot. Especially the year before she died. Actually, in the two weeks since she died we had gotten along better than ever before. Something about her not expecting sex, I think.

I parked as close as I could to the multiplex theater building and suddenly she was in a good mood again. She clapped her hands together and floated out of the car before I even had it stopped.

"I'm in heaven," she said, moving toward the ticket window.

I shook my head, muttering that she was a long way from heaven, but I certainly wished she would go there soon. I locked the car and checked twice to see if the hatch was shut tight and the blanket over her body was in place.

By the time I had bought my ticket to the show she wanted to see, she was already inside, floating in front of the popcorn counter, looking sad.

I moved up beside her and as softly as I could, without moving my lips, I asked, "What's wrong?"

She pointed at the popcorn.

"You knew you wouldn't be able to eat any?" I whispered.

She shook her head. "No, it's not that. I can pick it up and put it in my mouth." To demonstrate she took a piece from the counter and popped it into her mouth and chewed with her mouth half open. Thank god no one was watching.

"So what's the problem? And since when can you pick up stuff?"

She shrugged. "I've been doing that for days now. But I can't taste the popcorn."

More stupid ghost rules.

I stared at her for a moment and then glanced around the theater lobby to see if anyone was watching. Again we were in luck.

"Maybe I can find a Wizard spell to help you," I said. "Or maybe you'll just get better with practice." I regretted saying that immediately.

"Oh, you think so? Then get an extra large, extra butter. I'll practice all the way through the movie."

I was about to object when this couple moved up behind me and I was forced to get the guy behind the counter's attention and buy an extra large, extra butter popcorn and a small drink.

By the time I found her in the sixth theater down the hall the previews were already starting. I started to say something and she shushed me, just like she used to do when she was alive.

Dead. Alive. Nothing changes.

I balanced the popcorn on the rail between us and she began to eat handfuls, dropping exactly the same amount that she used to do when she was alive, only this time the dropped popcorn went through her and gathered in a pile on the seat. I'd have to ask her later how that worked and why I couldn't see the popcorn after it was inside her. More and more strange ghost rules.

I glanced around to see if anyone was watching or sitting close. We were in luck. This movie was a real dog and there were only five other people in the theater.

After every preview she leaned over and whispered that she wanted to see that movie, just like she had always done. And, as when she was alive, the thought made me shudder, but now for different reasons.

I spent most of the movie trying to work out plans of escape. I even thought of just going out of the theater and walking away. But I didn't have the guts to do that. Besides, eventually the police would find the car and her body and I would get caught. The life of a fugitive just wasn't one for me.

When the movie ended she sighed. "I really love movies."

"No kidding," I said under my breath and luckily she ignored me. I sat still, watching the credits and waiting until the other people left before standing.

"Too bad you couldn't just stay here."

Again she sighed. "That would be wonderful."

We headed out the back door near the screen in silence and it wasn't until I was at the car that I had realized what I had seen.

The multiplex theater's back door was right beside the screen. Under the screen, like in old theaters, was a stage, only this stage was fake, just used to get the screen up in the air. A maintenance man, or someone, must have left the access door open to the area under the stage, revealing rough planking on the floor spaced evenly over hard packed dirt.

There was nothing else under there and no reason for anyone to ever go under there.

"You really want to stay here?" I asked as she settled into her seat.

She looked at me with that questioning look, meaning she didn't understand. I always had liked that look because it meant she didn't understand something about me. She always took such pride in knowing everything about me, so that look had always cheered me up and tonight was no exception.

I pointed back at the closed door. "Go back through there and take a look under the stage."

"But—"

"Just do it." I loved having the upper hand.

She shrugged and floated/walked/moved toward the closed metal theater door and then through it like it was the surface of a lake.

A full minute later she was back, excited. "I see what you are thinking. You

---

could bury my body under the stage and I could see all the movies I wanted."

I nodded and she tried to hug me, which failed totally. But I suppose it was the thought that counted.

We went home, got my gloves and a shovel, and I tossed in my Wizards book just in case I might need it. We were back to the theater in less than an hour. I backed the car right up to the closest place I could get near the stage door and we waited until the next show ended and the people were leaving.

She went inside and stood guard and when she motioned that the coast was clear, I blocked the door open. As the credits were playing I got her body from the car and under the stage.

While she watched the movie again with eight live people, I buried her. I had to be real quiet, especially taking out and replacing the flooring planks. But I got it done, finishing the digging during the noisy love scene in the middle and then putting back the flooring during the loud chase scene at the end.

I did a quick Wizard invisibility blessing over her grave, then left the shovel in the back corner, as if it had been left by a workman. I went out behind the last movie-goer of the last show.

She met me in the car, smiling. "Thanks," she said.

I think that was the first time in years she had said that to me. I was taken aback. "My pleasure," was all I could think to say.

"Would you come tomorrow night and see a movie with me?"

"Sure," I said.

She clapped her hands together like a kid. "Great. You can buy me some popcorn."

"I'd be glad to," I said. And I really meant it. Since then I went to the movies there about once a week. No one ever talked about the ghost of the twelve-plex theater, except to complain about rude noises from empty seats behind them.

No one ever found her body.

I bought her popcorn every week and we never fought again. She seemed totally contented.

But after a few years I noticed she had this yellow tinge about her. I tried a Wizard curse to help her, but it did no good. I figured it was just too much yellow oil build-up.

～

## *Some Classic Dean Wesley Smith Stories*
### *Available at your favorite booksellers.*

# Coming in Two Months!!
## A Brand New Seeders Universe Novel
# STAR MIST

USA Today Bestselling Author

# DEAN WESLEY SMITH

# HEAVEN PAINTED
## *as a Cop Car*

A GHOST OF A CHANCE NOVELLA

*Eve Bryson died and found herself dead and lusting after a cop?*

*And not just any cop. Deputy McCall Cascade: Superhero.*

*Can a ghost and a superhero find true happiness and sex and stop a few killers along the way?*

*USA Today bestselling writer brings you the the fourth book in the crazy Ghost of a Chance series?*

# HEAVEN PAINTED AS A COP CAR
## *A Ghost of a Chance Novella*

## ONE

**EVE BRYSON DIED** so fast, she didn't even realize she was dead for a few minutes.

The rain was pounding down hard, one of those storms that felt more like standing under a cold shower. She had on only a light cotton summer dress, sandals, and panties. No bra, so this rain was sticking her dress to her like a second skin. Not pleasant in the slightest.

Around her the heavy pine forest seemed frighteningly dark, even though the sun was hours from setting. She could hear nothing but the pounding rain against her head, matting her long brown hair into a mess down her back.

She wasn't even sure how she had ended up in the rain. A moment before she had been driving toward a dinner date at a local brewpub in downtown Portland with three friends from college.

In the years since college, the four of them had managed to get together every month or so and she loved those evenings. It took her mind off her worthless husband and even more worthless job she couldn't figure out how to get out of.

She had thought she would love high-tech work after coming out of college with her masters in engineering. But she hated it, hated the people more than anything else. Their goal wasn't to create new things, use their brains for good. All they did was try to figure out how to get ahead in the corporate game.

And just like her job, she thought marrying Simpson Jones right out of college was a good idea as well. It didn't matter that he was taking a break from finishing his degree. They had had great sex, lots of fun traveling, and planning for a future. She thought she had found a soul mate.

Maybe a soul mate for her single lost sock. But that might be giving Simpson more credit than he deserved.

It seemed good ol' Simp to his friends never understood that working was required to get ahead. She had no idea what he did all day while she was working, but it certainly wasn't anything to bring in money. She had a hunch he just looked at porn and played online games. She had gotten tired of asking about six months ago.

The marriage was that dead.

So for two years now she had supported him and that was going to end very, very soon. All of the rebel things she had found charming with him in college now just annoyed her beyond belief.

And all of her friends didn't like him either right from the start. That should have been a clue to her, but when a girl was in the first blush of love and sexual satisfaction, thinking with the logical brain wasn't that possible.

So she had made two mistakes right out of college. In six months, she would be out of both mistakes.

She shivered from the pounding cold rain and looked around. What had happened?

The two-lane winding road through the trees was empty. Water ran down one side, it was raining so hard.

Then she saw her wonderful little classic blue Miata off the road and down an embankment. Then she remembered. She had been thinking about how Simpson had complained that she wouldn't cook his dinner before she left. She had gotten so angry, she had been driving far too fast down the twisting area through the trees from their house in the hills to the main street below.

Far too fast for a pounding June rain.

She had slid into one corner, managed to get straightened out, and then didn't make the next corner. The last thing she remembered was the Miata heading over the bank and for a large pine tree.

She must have bumped her head. She didn't remember climbing up here to the road.

She quickly felt her forehead, looking for any sign of blood in the rain pounding at her.

Nothing.

The Miata's lights were still on and she went to the edge of the road to look down at it. It was pretty smashed up, but it wasn't that far off the road and the next person to come by would certainly see it and her.

She felt really sad she had totaled her Miata. She had bought it right out of college as well and it was the only fun thing left in her life after two years. Now it looked like she would be starting over completely.

The rain kept pounding at her and she could feel she was starting to really get chilled. It had been a seventy-degree day today. How could she be this cold?

A blue pickup, brand new from the looks of it, came around the corner, saw the lights from her car and quickly braked and pulled over onto the gravel shoulder of the road, putting on its flashing red warning lights.

The driver was a guy about forty. Maybe older. She could never tell with men in that range.

He pulled on a rain jacket with a hood as he climbed out and went to the edge of the road to look at her poor car.

She put one arm across her chest to cover what was showing through her wet dress and said to the guy, "I sure made a mess of it, didn't I?"

He said nothing, but instead quickly scrambled down the bank. When he got to the Miata, he looked inside, then shook his head and at a fast climb came back up the bank and started toward his truck.

"Why are you ignoring me?" Eve asked.

She reached for the guy as he went past and her hand went right through his arm.

And as it did, she could feel and read his mind.

All he was thinking was to get help out here quickly. And that he doubted the woman in the car was alive. Her neck was badly twisted in a way that necks didn't twist.

She watched him move to the truck and climb in and use his cell phone to call for help.

Then in the pounding rain, she moved over to the edge of the bank and once again looked at her car.

She could see now that she was still inside.

She was dead.

And she was just about as cold and wet as she could ever remember being. And she was getting hungry.

She was dead.

She was a ghost.

How the hell could she be hungry?

# TWO

**DEPUTY MCCALL CASCADE** flat hated this part of his job. For two years now he had been working as a deputy sheriff. Except for the paperwork, he liked the job.

And he was good at it, actually.

But going to fatality crash sites was not anything he liked to do. Why would he? There was no one left to help.

He eased his patrol car over to the side of the road, but about four car lengths from the actual crash site since an ambulance was already taking up a part of that area. He turned on his lights to warn drivers coming down the winding hill.

He had also set flares back up the road. This road didn't have that much traffic, but in this pouring rain, he could see why someone would go off the road if not paying attention or driving too fast for the wet, slick pavement.

He pulled up the hood on his rain slicker against the hard, pouring and damned cold rain and climbed out, leaving his car running to stay warm and for all the computer equipment to keep running. Joining the force two years ago, he had been surprised at the amount of computer work they had to do.

He moved down to where the two ambulance attendants in yellow rain slickers were already going down to the wreck. He went over the edge to join them.

It was an instant verdict by both attendants. The young woman driving the blue Miata had died instantly on impact.

Cascade decided he didn't need to look. He didn't need the image in his mind. He had become a cop to help people, not stare at dead bodies.

He had the attendants get her purse and put it in a plastic bag. Then he headed back up the embankment to where the man who had reported the accident stood.

"She's dead, isn't she?" the man asked.

Cascade nodded.

"Damn," the guy said, shaking his head.

Cascade agreed with that completely. Thankfully she had been the only one in the car.

Cascade took the guy's name and address and thanked him for calling in the crash. Then he let the guy go, noting his license plate on his blue truck as the guy drove away.

Then Cascade turned to head back to his car and to find out the identity of the poor young woman in the mangled car below. It was going to take a while for all the angles of the accident to be photographed and her body removed from the car. Thankfully, none of that was his job.

He got back into his warm patrol car and dug out the woman's purse from the plastic bag, then her wallet inside the purse, and then her driver's license.

He sort of jerked as he saw her picture. She had been very attractive, with long brown hair, brown eyes, and a really nice smile that made her eyes seem to almost sparkle.

And she was his age.

"Too damn young," he said out loud, feeling a wave of sadness wash over him.

In the back of his mind he thought he heard a woman's voice say "Thanks."

He glanced around and then shook his head and pushed down his hood on his slicker and logged the information into his computer. This was just a tragedy, a horrible tragedy that there was no way he could have prevented.

A moment later he heard a woman's voice say in the distance, "Holy shit, someone who actually cares."

He again glanced around, but there was no one, of course. Maybe this was another of his superpowers that he didn't know much about.

He had agreed to become a superhero in the law enforcement division of the world. It seemed that everything that existed had a god around it and there were lots of superheroes around in most areas to try to help people.

He had no idea at all what becoming a superhero meant, other than she said he would no longer age and his natural talents would become more pronounced as time went on and he got control of his powers.

He had no idea he had powers. But he had to admit, he saw things other cops didn't notice and he could almost read a person's emotions.

Reanna, his boss in the law enforcement side of superheroes, had told him he had lots of time to learn.

He just wasn't sure what he was supposed to be learning.

And sitting in front of a tragedy where a young person died far too early in life sure wasn't teaching him anything. That he was sure about.

He shook his head and started to get out of the patrol car when he heard the voice again.

"Mr. Perfect."

He ignored it and closed the door and went back to help with getting the young woman's body out of the car.

He didn't feel like Mr. Perfect.

In fact, far, far from it at the moment.

# THREE

**AFTER STARING AT** her car for a moment in the pouring rain, Eve had managed to find a tree on the inside of the road to give herself some shelter from the rain. But by the time the first cop arrived, she had been shivering so bad, she doubted she could even walk.

Was it possible to die twice, once from a car crash, another from freezing to death?

One of the county sheriffs left his car running when he climbed out in his rain slicker. So she had gone over to his car and tried to open the back-seat car door, but her hand went right through it.

"Shit!" she had shouted into the rain. "Just shit."

She needed to do something, so she closed her eyes and just pretended she was going to climb into the back seat. She wouldn't have been surprised if she had ended up sitting on the concrete, but she actually ended up in the back seat of the car.

Success.

She could go through a door, but not fall through a seat. Who knew?

And thankfully, the sheriff had the heater running on defrost to keep the windows clear, so it was warm in the car.

He had a towel beside his seat and she had grabbed it, coming away with what felt like a towel in her hands, but the

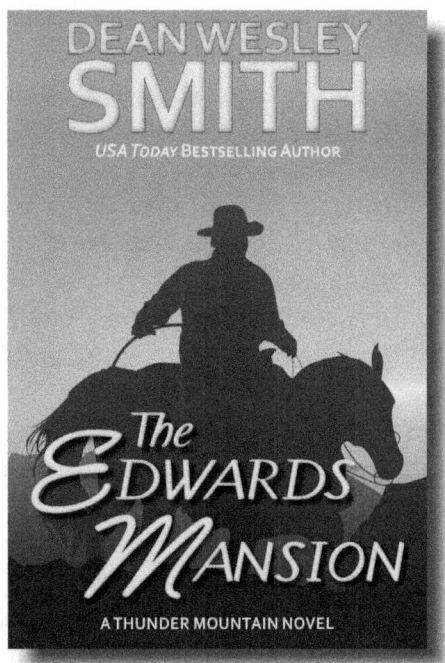

original towel remained in position. The one in her hand looked identical.

She hadn't cared. Ghost towel or not, it was a towel.

Since she was a ghost, she had figured no one could see her, so she had stripped off her soaked dress and underwear and used the towel to dry off. Then she had finally used the towel to wrap up her wet hair on the top of her head.

She twisted the water out of her underwear and slid them under her butt to protect herself a little from the cold seat.

Then she twisted as much water out of her dress that she could and draped it over the front passenger seat to dry.

She was finally starting to warm up. She was naked and sitting in the back of a cop car. Under any other circumstances than being dead, this might have caused nightmares.

It still might.

The evening was just getting started.

Suddenly, the cop climbed back into his car. He was holding her purse in a plastic bag and as she watched, he pulled out her purse, then her wallet, then her driver's license and shook his head.

"Too damn young."

"Thanks," she said from the back seat.

He pushed his raincoat hood off the back of his head and she gasped. Sheriff man was about her age and a looker, with short brown hair, a square chin, and from what she saw in the rearview mirror, bright green eyes.

And she instantly noticed he wasn't wearing a ring.

What the hell was wrong with her? She was dead and lusting after a cop?

She stared at him for a moment as he called in her personal information and then keyed into the keyboard even more

information, running her driver's license through a scanner.

She was impressed. One high-tech car.

Then he just sat waiting for even more information to come up on his computer screen.

She really wanted to know more about this guy. Dead or not, a girl could look, couldn't she?

Maybe if she touched him, she could read his mind like she had done with the guy who found her wreck.

She reached forward and put her hand on his shoulder.

Only her hand went inside him and she instantly felt the sadness he was feeling at her death.

"Holy shit, someone who actually cares," she said aloud.

He glanced around, making her pull back and cover herself.

Then he shook his head and went back to studying the information coming through her screen.

"Can I make someone hear me if I am touching them? How cool would that be?"

He didn't turn around at that, so she reached forward and once again put her hand inside his shoulder.

This time she let herself try to find out who he was before saying anything.

His name was Deputy McCall Cascade. Everyone just called him Cascade.

She liked that name.

He was exactly her age at twenty-six, liked his job except for events like this. He liked helping people and he didn't have a girlfriend.

But there was even more. He really worked as a superhero in the law enforcement area under a woman who was a low-level god in law enforcement by the name of Reanna. She reported to some gods above her, but he had never met any of them.

She had no idea what the superhero thinking was. Some sort of game or something. He was new at it, only being recruited by the gods of law enforcement two years before right after he had joined the force.

"Mr. Perfect," she said aloud with her hand still in his shoulder.

She could tell he had heard that.

He shook his head, put up his raincoat hood and climbed back out into the rain as another sheriff's car arrived followed by a second ambulance.

Wow, she was worth two ambulances. Thankfully she wouldn't be paying the bill on this one.

She watched for the next thirty minutes as they got her body out of the car and up into the second ambulance.

The more she sat there, the more puzzled she got by all of this. She had no idea what was going on.

She had never believed in ghosts or an afterlife or anything. But clearly she was living, at least for the moment, some sort of afterlife.

And she was hungry and pretty soon would need to pee.

You would think a ghost wouldn't have to deal with all the real world stuff. Rules of ghostiness were sure different from anything she had ever read or watched in the movies.

Twenty minutes later, Cascade climbed back into the patrol car and again lowered the hood on his raincoat.

Her breath caught, if she had been breathing, which she was pretty certain she had been. He had gotten even more handsome, if that was possible.

He moved her purse in its plastic bag from the console beside him to the passenger seat, then waited until the ambulance in front of him pulled away. He pulled out to follow it. It seemed he had gotten the duty of staying with her body.

If she had been alive, he could have done more to her body than just stay with it.

Then she laughed.

If he could actually see her in the back seat, sitting nude on her still damp panties, wouldn't he be surprised?

Actually, come to think of it, she was the one sitting here that was surprised.

She had expected a great night with friends.

She hadn't expected to die.

But she supposed no one expected to die.

She actually wasn't that upset about it for some reason. But she really needed to pee.

# FOUR

**CASCADE DROVE** behind the ambulance as they worked their way down the dark, tree-lined canyon and to one of the main roads. Neither he nor the ambulance had emergency lights on since there was no reason to be in a hurry.

Eve Bryson was in the ambulance and there was no doubt she was dead.

He just couldn't take his mind off the smiling picture of Eve on her driver's license. He had a sense that if he had known her, he would have liked her. Of course, that wouldn't have mattered since she was married and he never allowed himself to get near any married woman.

Actually, in the last few years, he had only dated a few times. He liked his solitude, mostly. And just hadn't found anyone that really attracted him.

Or that he felt a connection with in any form.

Eve's picture had attracted him, and he had felt an attraction to her. But maybe that was because she was safe.

She was dead.

And he had no idea where the voice was coming from he was hearing. That had never happened before. He was going to have to ask Reanna about that next time he talked with her. He wasn't certain if hearing voices was a superpower or a sign he was going crazy.

He didn't feel crazy. And the woman's voice in his head sure sounded sane as well.

Anything was possible, he was starting to learn. As a regular Marine and then four years of college, he had had no idea about any of this superpower and superhero stuff. No regular person did.

And now that he was starting to learn about it, he sure didn't talk about it to anyone. They would lock him away and toss the key into the brush.

That was another reason he hadn't found anyone to really care about. Supposedly he was going to live a long time. How could he tell a partner that he was a superhero and got his instructions from the gods of law enforcement? Not the best grounds for any kind of relationship.

He pulled into an area off the back of the hospital behind the ambulance. Damn he hated this. But it needed to be done.

As the two ambulance attendants got out and went to unload Eve's body, Cascade sighed.

He picked up her purse and his clipboard and ignoring the woman's voice in his head talking about regret, he got out to follow the body into the hospital.

He wanted to rescue people. Stop bad guys.

Not follow dead people around.

Parts of this job most certainly sucked.

# FIVE

**EVE HAD NO** idea why the ambulance took her body to a hospital. She was clearly dead and they weren't even bothering to run with lights.

So as they pulled into a hospital loading area, she touched Deputy Cascade again.

The answer she was looking for came easily. Because she died alone and under suspicious circumstances, they had to do an autopsy. And it seemed in this county, the hospital morgue was where that was done.

"You won't find anything in my bloodstream except anger and a lot of regret."

She could see in his mind that he heard her. He wasn't certain what he was hearing, but he clearly heard what she had said.

He picked up her purse and she grabbed her dress. They were parked under a canopy so she wouldn't get wet. She closed her eyes and pretended to open the door and step out of the back seat of the car.

The evening air had a chill to it and she was in front of a hospital, naked except for sandals on her feet and a towel wrapped on her head. Now this was the stuff of nightmares.

She quickly slipped her still-damp dress over her head. That sent shivers down her spine. But it was better than walking around a hospital completely naked.

Slightly better.

If there were other ghosts, she was going to make a great first impression. A dress you could see through and a towel on her head.

Cascade was striding toward the big double doors, following the gurney with her body on it.

She ran and caught up to him, going through the wide sliding-glass door beside him. Inside, the dim hallway smelled of antiseptic and roses, of all things.

The gurney with her body on it sort of clicked going down the smooth tile floor and she walked beside Cascade.

She just felt right walking beside him. Weird, but true.

In this part of the hospital, there sure weren't a lot of people.

But as her body turned to the right toward a service elevator, Cascade turned left and went through two swinging doors and out into a much more active and brighter area of the hospital.

Nurses and doctors were moving around, along with patients and guests. Cascade seemed to know where he was going with her purse and the paperwork on his clipboard, so she just tagged along, trying to stay out of everyone's way, since none of them could see her.

And she almost succeeded in that task except for one man who came around a corner carrying a dozen roses. He had a dark look to his eyes and wore jeans, a T-shirt, and tennis shoes.

She went right through him before she really saw him.

And as she did, she saw why he was here.

His name was Jack Nevada and he was headed for a room she and Cascade had passed down the hall. Hidden in the roses he had a syringe that he was going to inject in a woman by the name of Stephanie to kill her. It would look like a natural death.

He was a paid killer, hired by Stephanie's husband.

"Holy shit!"

Eve froze in the hallway, watching Jack Nevada stroll toward his murder victim.

"What the hell! What the hell! What the hell!"

No one heard her.

What could she do? She was a ghost. She couldn't shout or even try to stop the guy.

She glanced back in the other direction.

Deputy Cascade, gun and all, had stopped at the nurse's station and was smiling at a young nurse in front of him.

Eve had to tell him, somehow.

She ran toward Cascade, her sandals slapping on the tile. She tried to stop before she got to him, but instead slid and went right inside him.

He stood up straight as she did.

She liked it inside the big tall hunk of a man.

"Hi, handsome," she said. "Eve Bryson here inside you in ghost form. We got a problem that you need to solve real quick!"

He nodded to the nurse and stepped back, which made Eve smile. Even under stress of hearing voices, he could stay cool. This guy really was a superhero.

"I am, actually," he said out loud.

Some guy in a white smock looked at him and frowned.

"No need to talk in your out loud voice," she said. "I can hear everything you are thinking."

She felt him panic and she laughed.

"Yes, even the fact that you thought I was hot. Thank you, by the way."

He took a deep breath.

"So what do you need?" he thought at her.

She described the guy she had touched and what room he was headed toward and what he was about to do."

"Shit!" he said, again out loud. "Are you sure?"

"One hundred percent," she said to him. "And if you want to save that woman's life you had better get this handsome hunk of a body moving."

Damn, this ghost thing was getting better and better by the moment if she could be inside other people.

He touched the counter in front of the nurse. "Security to room 1003. Stat!"

He turned and started at a run toward the room, using his mike attached to his collar to call for backup of real police.

When he reached the room, he drew his gun.

She sent him calming thoughts.

"Thanks," he said.

Then he went inside, gun drawn, leaving the door standing open for backup to come in behind him.

The killer had put the roses down near the window and had a syringe in his right hand. He was working with the woman's IV and in another fifteen seconds would have injected her.

Eve had given Cascade a clear image of who the man was and what he was planning.

The woman under the blanket was a very large woman. And the room smelled like she had had an accident in the sheets.

"Step back and drop the syringe and put your hands in the air!" Cascade said.

Cascade's power and authority in his voice gave Eve little goose bumps. He could order her around like that any time he wanted.

"Trying to work here," he said in his silent voice.

"Sorry," she said, laughing. "Forgot where I was."

The man with the syringe looked shocked at the deputy and gun facing him.

The man took a step back.

"No worry," she said to Cascade. "He's not armed with anything but the needle."

"I said drop the needle and put your hands on your head."

The guy finally realized he had no options, so he dropped the syringe with a light click on the tile, then raised his hands.

At that moment two hospital security men came through the door.

"Needle on the floor," Cascade said to the security. "He was about to inject this woman with it. Hired kill I'm betting."

Cascade handed one of the security men his handcuffs. "Secure his hands behind his back."

The security man did and Cascade had the would-be killer sit on the floor with his back against a wall.

Then one of the security men used a tissue to pick up the syringe.

At that point, two police officers came through the door and the shit-smelling room got real crowded real quick.

"You're going to be busy," Eve said to Cascade. "I'm going to leave you for a bit."

"You coming back?" he asked in his inside voice.

"I think so," she said. "But I'm still new at this ghost stuff."

"So where are you going?"

"You don't know?" she asked.

"Not a clue."

"I've really got to pee."

"Ghosts pee?" he asked.

"I'm going to find out for the first time very, very shortly," she said.

And with that she stepped out of his body.

She felt almost empty not being with him.

She worked her way out of the room to find a woman's rest room. She doubted the hospital had ghost rest rooms.

But who knew.

## SIX

**CASCADE FELT MORE** alone than he had ever felt in his life without Eve's spirit or ghost or whatever inside him. She had filled parts of him he hadn't known were missing.

And now he had to suck it up and take on the business of being a sheriff.

First, he had to be in the poor woman's smelly room while everything was photographed and he walked through what had happened.

He had said he had caught a glimpse of the syringe in the roses when he passed the man walking in, decided it could be nothing but bad.

Eve had suggested that story before she left him to find a bathroom, since he pretty much couldn't tell anyone he had a ghost inside him helping him.

And since he had drawn his gun, there was paperwork for that as well. He had to explain why he had drawn his gun and what he was thinking and everything.

Then he still had the task of checking in Eve's body, which took even more time.

He kept hoping Eve was still around, but she never touched him to let him

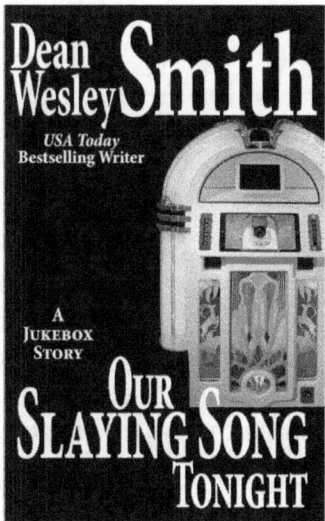

*Some Classic Dean Wesley Smith Stories*
*Available at your favorite booksellers.*

know if she was or wasn't and he didn't hear her voice.

When she had been inside him, he had realized that when he started hearing her voice, she was actually naked in the back seat of his patrol car. That thought just made him smile.

Finally, he managed to get out of the hospital and down to headquarters where he had to spend even more time filling out paperwork there.

He didn't mind the paperwork when it meant he had saved a life. And thanks to Eve, this evening he had.

Now, somehow, he just hoped Eve was still around.

And then, as he was heading for his car to go home, she touched him.

And he could feel her and her presence was with him and that just made him smile once again.

# SEVEN

**IT TOOK DEPUTY** Cascade two hours to fill out the paperwork on Eve's body and on the arrest at the hospital.

She had raided a candy machine for a few snacks by just sticking her hand through the glass and pulling out the ghost equivalent of a candy bar. The two bars helped a little to hold back the hunger, but she was going to need a real meal pretty soon.

Amazing how two candy bars could taste so damned good. Sort of like that first lick from an ice cream cone combined with the first bite into a perfect steak.

Heavenly.

Cascade then had to spend another thirty minutes at his desk at the police station filling out more paperwork before he could get off work. Wow did cops have a lot of paperwork or what? She had no idea.

She just sat off to one side and watched, admiring his wonderful body and handsome face.

She was a ghost, yet she had needed to pee and clearly now needed to eat. What rule said she couldn't lust after a live cop?

So as Cascade finally stood and started for his patrol car, she got back inside him.

"How you doing?"

"I was wondering if you were still here."

She could tell that he had missed her. As much as she had missed him.

This was getting interesting.

"Been watching the entire time," she said. "I figured if I was inside your body, I would just be a distraction to all the stuff you needed to get done."

"More than likely yes," he said.

And she could tell he appreciated that, even though he had missed her.

"Dinner at Shari's," she said.

"Ghosts eat and pee?"

"It seems we do," Eve said, laughing. "I need to eat because I'm ravished and the two wonderful candy bars won't hold me much longer. I died on my way to meet friends for dinner."

"I am so sorry to hear that," he said, suddenly feeling very sad.

"For some reason I'm not," she said.

So fifteen minutes later they were in Shari's restaurant.

This Shari's was like any other Shari's restaurant. Maroon cloth and wood tones and lots of booths with tall wood walls between them. The place was known for great pies and they always had them in cases as you walked in.

Eve had just wanted to stick her hand inside one of the cases and grab pie and shove it in her mouth. That was how hungry she was. Somehow she managed to not do that, acting as if she was alive and following Cascade to a booth in the back next to a window.

She sat across the booth from him so she could see him, but she put her feet up so that they were in his lap, so she could be inside his head and he could hear her.

She told him how she was sitting.

"Kind of forward, don't you think?" he said, smiling.

Damn from across the table, she loved that smile.

"Thank you," he said, hearing her thought about his smile.

Then as the waitress came up, he ordered his regular French Dip and fries and a glass of iced tea.

"I'm going to go get something," she said. "Back in a moment."

She wandered into the kitchen and there, sitting under the light ready to take out, was a wonderful chicken fried steak meal. It smelled heavenly.

She picked up the plate, feeling the heat on her fingers.

The real plate just stayed there under the light. It seemed food had a ghost component as well, just as the candy bars did in the machine.

She took the plate back out to the table, put her foot against his leg and said, "I have chicken fried steak. So pardon me if you get moaning sensations as I eat. I'm that hungry."

She took a couple of bites, then realized while she was gone, he had called for his boss on the superhero side.

Just as Eve realized that, a striking black-haired woman in a police uniform came up to the table. She had to stand a good six feet tall and her uniform looked like it had actually been starched.

The woman nodded in Eve's direction and then had Cascade scoot over.

Eve moved so she could keep her foot in contact with Cascade.

"This is Reanna," Cascade thought at her.

"Figured as much," Eve said between bites.

This had to be the absolute best-tasting chicken fried steak she had ever had. Ever.

"I understand you just died this afternoon," Reanna said out loud to Eve. "Sorry for your loss, but glad you could help Deputy Cascade."

"Tell her it was my pleasure," Eve said out loud. "Ask her if she wants me to touch her so she can hear me."

"I can see and hear you just fine," Reanna said.

Then Reanna waved a hand in the direction of Cascade.

He blinked and then said to Eve, "Wow you are more beautiful alive than dead."

"Thanks," Eve said, "I think."

At that moment, she realized her dress was still damp, more than likely her nipples were still showing, and she still had her hair wrapped up on top of her head in his car towel. "I got a little wet out there at the crash site."

Then she ignored the feelings of attraction she was getting from Cascade through their touch and looked at Reanna. "If I'm a ghost, how can you see me? And how can Cascade now see me?"

"You are a ghost agent," Reanna said, her voice firm and compact, just as she looked. "You will be recruited to join the Ghost of a Chance Agency and trained by them."

"You lost me with ghost agent thingie," Eve said.

"When a person dies," Reanna said, "almost everyone just goes on into the next life, whatever that is. But for a few thousand around the world, they are asked to stay on as ghost agents and try to help people, as you two did by saving that woman's life this evening."

Eve nodded. "That did feel good."

"I have contacted the head of the Ghost of a Chance agency," Reanna said, "and they will be sending some other agents to help you train and explain everything to you."

Eve nodded, but her disappointment matched what she was feeling from Cascade.

"However," Reanna said, "after your collaboration this afternoon with Officer Cascade, I have also asked if you could be assigned to my department and you and Officer Cascade work together to solve cases."

Reanna turned to Cascade. "Would that would be all right with you?"

"I would be honored," he said.

Eve could feel his excitement at the idea. And she had to admit that hanging around with Mister Handsome Superhero sounded like a great time to her.

"Would you be interested in such an assignment?" Reanna asked Eve. "You both would be a very special team, the only ghost agent and live superhero working together. It has never been tried. You might work with Poker Boy and his team at times as well as reporting to me. He was very interested in meeting you both once you are up to speed."

She instantly felt Cascade's excitement. It seemed this superhero named Poker Boy and his team often were called on to save the entire world.

So Eve had a chance to go from a worthless husband and a dead job to being someone who could help save people and work with superheroes and gods.

Not counting staying with the hunk of a man sitting across from her. She had no idea how she would figure out the sex problem, but given time, and work, she imagined it might be possible.

How could she say no to that?

"I would be honored," she said out loud.

Reanna smiled and nodded.

Cascade's excitement at her answer sent tingles to places she hadn't felt tingles in a very long time.

Damn, this being dead was going to be a blast.

Who knew?

# PART TWO
*A Really, Really Bad Guy*

# EIGHT

**EVE BRYSON WAS DEAD.**

She knew that for sure now and liked it more than being alive. And now after a month or so, she was getting used to all the perks that came with being dead.

She had avoided anything to do with her funeral and her ex-husband and her old life. She was dead. Even though she was still hanging around the world of the living, she had moved on.

And she had a crush on Deputy McCall Cascade.

# Now Available
## from all your favorite booksellers in trade paper and electronic editions.

USA TODAY BESTSELLING AUTHOR

# DEAN WESLEY SMITH

# THE HIGH EDGE

A SEEDERS UNIVERSE NOVEL

More than a crush, actually. She was in lust with him and maybe falling in love with him. Sometimes the two sort of got mixed up.

So even though she had been in Las Vegas training for a month, they had continued to learn about each other as much as they could.

For Eve, the training with two other Ghost of a Chance agents had gone great.

And she had discovered that ghosts had some pretty nifty powers.

For example, she knew how to be inside another person and control that living person. She would never do that with Cascade, but she sure could do it to normal people and who knew when that would come in handy.

And she could teleport anywhere she wanted to go. That allowed her to check in with Cascade during her training every day. They had dinner together every night and both of them loved it.

She got to hear about his day, he got to hear about her training. She loved having someone to talk to.

With the help of a few other superheroes, including the famous Poker Boy and his girlfriend Patty, Eve had her own condo in the Pearl district of Portland.

When Eve had asked how they could do that, Patty had told her that they were so rich they didn't know what to do with all their money, so they could use it as a tax shelter by buying a condo and then not renting it to anyone alive.

Patty and Sherrie, another superhero, even helped Eve furnish her condo the way she wanted it so she had her own place, with dishes, a toilet seat without a lid, and everything.

The other ghost agents found it great that she was working with a superhero as a partner.

A live superhero.

Something very different.

As one of them said, she was doing something that had never been tried before in thousands and thousands of years.

It was going to be interesting to see how it worked out.

Up until a few weeks ago, she didn't even know that any of this ghost and superhero world even existed. But she had to admit, being dead and being a ghost agent was a lot better than being alive and being with the worthless husband she had been stupid enough to marry. She didn't miss him or her old crappy job at all.

Not even for a passing second, which when she thought about it, was very sad. Her living life had been pathetic.

And she really didn't miss being alive in the slightest. This was much, much better.

One of the very weird things about being dead was that the food tasted better. Everything around her seemed more alive as well, and from what one of the other ghost agents had hinted at, the sex was better too.

With other ghost agents.

But she was far, far more interested in having sex with Cascade.

And he seemed to be interested in her as well. He had a smile that could melt the paint off a freeway sign at a half-mile and she loved just sitting across from him over dinner and seeing that smile.

And he said, and she believed him since she could read his thoughts when she wanted, that he loved her long brown hair, her button nose that others found cute and she found sort of weird, and her blue eyes.

She only came up to his chest in height, but since very few people could see them both, that made no difference at all.

The biggest thing was that she could make him laugh and he liked that.

And she loved watching him laugh.

Since she had been inside his head, she knew he liked her, was attracted to her, wanted to be with her. They just hadn't figured out the logistics of a relationship yet between superhero and ghost. If she had anything to say about it, they would.

Especially the sex part.

It might take time. Both of them had all the time in the world.

She was dead, he was basically immortal.

Worked out perfectly.

# NINE

**CASCADE HAD REALLY** missed Eve during her days away training in Las Vegas. So he had focused on just learning more about the job as deputy sheriff and also more about being a superhero.

He and Reanna had talked a few times. One lunch at a small café with little traffic and decent sandwiches, they had had a great conversation. They had moved out onto an open patio so no one could overhear them. The day wasn't hot yet, but it was warming up quickly. Reanna even took off her hat for the first time since he had known her.

She had longer hair than he had thought she had, but it had been tucked up under her hat and pinned there.

Over a grilled ham and cheese, he had been surprised to find out that he was fairly unique. That only about ten superheroes worked in law enforcement around the United States and less than one hundred total around the world.

"We can't help everyone," Reanna had said as she worked at her club sandwich. "But we try to recruit superheroes like you in critical areas and the Portland area is a critical area into the future."

She didn't explain why and Cascade hadn't pushed.

"I'll have Screamer, who is one of our superheroes and working with Poker Boy at times, come and talk with you. He's a Las Vegas detective."

"Screamer?" Cascade had asked.

"A nickname that has just stuck," Reanna said. "He can read minds and connect two people in thoughts through him. He can also plant images in people's minds and one day got a really nasty slime-ball to give up a location of where he had buried a young girl alive by putting horror images in the guy's mind and making him scream."

"Am I going to be able to do things like that?" Cascade asked, not really sure he liked the idea of making people scream. Not his style.

Reanna had shrugged. "Everyone develops their own powers in their own time. No telling what you will be able to do. Give it time."

The only thing he could do was just nod at that and go back to eating.

After a week of Eve being gone, she appeared in front of him one day while he was eating lunch at Denny's. She was smiling and looking worried at the same time.

"Be right back," she said, looking around and laughing.

Then she vanished again.

Two minutes later she was back, really smiling. "I can teleport anywhere I want!"

He laughed at the excitement in her voice.

"I'm learning a lot," she had said. "You up for dinner tonight?"

"I would love that," he had said. "My place."

And after that, every night for the rest of the month or so of her training, they had had dinner together.

And that made him missing her feel a little less intense.

But when she jumped away every evening to go back to her hotel room in Las Vegas, his apartment once again felt empty.

He had no idea how he could miss a ghost as much as he did.

But there was no doubt how he felt about her.

No doubt in the slightest.

# TEN

**EVE WAS SO** glad that Cascade's boss in the superhero land had given him the power to see and hear her. And so in public all they had to do was be careful that he wasn't seen talking to himself too much, since no one else could see her.

To solve that problem, he had gotten a thin microphone that extended from an earpiece. She had laughed when she saw it and wished she could kiss him for being so smart. Now if someone did see him talking to her, that person would think he was just talking into his microphone.

The only other thing they had to be careful of was the dash camera inside his patrol car when he made stops. That was the only time it came on.

On her first full day back from training with the other ghost agents, she and Cascade had figured it would be a good

idea for her to just ride along with him on a standard patrol.

She liked that idea. Neither of them was sure how this "working together" was going to be, so a standard patrol day seemed like a logical place to start.

The first time she had ridden with him in the patrol car to the restaurant, sitting there beside him had felt right to her.

The patrol car smelled faintly of his soap combined with a leather smell from his belt and a computer smell from the equipment between the seats. She liked this car. It had been her refuge from the rain after her car wreck the first hour she was a ghost.

Now she felt comfortable in the front seat beside him, sitting in her jeans and white blouse, her hair pulled back.

He was in his full uniform, blue with dark trim, with a wide-brimmed hat just behind him on the floor between the seats so he could grab it easily.

The Portland July weather was only in the 80s, with bright sun promising to warm up the afternoon.

They had started their patrol at seven in the morning, and since there were no cameras or microphones in the car unless they were stopping someone or in pursuit, they chatted about her training, about the few other ghost agents she had met, and so on.

Then a half-hour into the ride, he saw a speeder in a blue Ford sedan passing cars in a no-passing area.

"There's an accident waiting to happen," she said.

"Let's see if we can stop it from happening," he said, flipping on his lights and pulling out after the speeder.

At that point the inside camera and microphone were working, so he had to be careful, but she could talk to him out loud just fine, since no one but him could hear her.

As he pulled out after the speeder, Cascade tapped a button on his steering wheel and on the computer screen she could see he was connected to his dispatcher.

Through a shorthand form of talking that she really needed to learn, he gave their location and what he was after and where the speeder was heading.

Eve had never been in a car chasing another car before.

It felt weird.

And exhilarating.

It would have been scary, but nothing could hurt her. So instead she worried about Cascade.

But it was clear he was an expert driver. And very comfortable behind the wheel. Maybe that was one of his superpowers. She would have to ask.

The moment the blue Ford saw Cascade's flashing lights, it signaled and pulled over, sliding to a stop in the gravel shoulder of the highway.

"Guy is in a hurry somewhere," Eve said.

Cascade pulled in behind him, reporting their position.

"Give me a moment to check it out," Eve said.

She knew that cops walking up to a car were in a lot of danger. So she liked how this could be part of her job with him, and help keep him a little safer in a dangerous job.

She went out through the door and up to the driver's side. What she saw through the driver's window shocked her for a moment.

The guy was a young man, sweating, and clearly scared, his eyes round and his breathing rushed. And slouched down in the passenger seat beside him was a very pregnant wife who was also sweating and shouting in pain. The woman's black hair looked like it was glued to her head.

From the way she was sitting with her legs splayed open and her nightshirt up, she looked to be about to pop a kid right onto the floor mat.

"Shit, just shit!" Eve said and waved for Cascade to hurry.

He got out of the patrol car, walked at a fast pace up beside Eve.

He took one look at the scene and said to the driver. "Can she make it?"

Oh, shit. Eve couldn't help deliver a baby. She was a ghost and wouldn't have a clue what to do anyway.

"I think so," the guy said, glancing at the woman.

"Hurry!" the woman shouted and then screamed in pain.

Eve at that moment was counting her lucky stars she had never been pregnant. That did not look like fun in the slightest.

"Stay on my bumper all the way."

"Thank you, officer," the young, soon-to-be-father said.

Cascade and Eve both ran back to the patrol car and with lights flashing and sirens cutting through the morning air, Cascade pulled out and the blue Ford did the same, staying right with Cascade as he drove and reported in what was happening, alerting the hospital to stand ready.

Six minutes later at the closest hospital, the blue Ford was met with a doctor, a couple nurses, and a stretcher. The almost-mother was rushed inside.

From what Eve could tell, they made it with minutes to spare. That kid really wanted to be born.

Cascade smiled at Eve as they climbed back into the cruiser. "Now that's the kind of thing I wish would happen more often."

"Nice way to start my first day on the job," Eve said, taking a deep breath and relaxing. Just helping a couple get to the hospital had stressed her.

But it was a great way to start the day.

She felt great. And right at that moment she knew she was going to like this job for far more reasons than just being with a hunk of a superhero.

Although, that sure didn't hurt.

# ELEVEN

**CASCADE REALLY LIKED** the fact that Eve had been able to go up and take a look at the situation in a stopped car. Not only had it saved time today and got a woman in labor to a hospital on time, but Cascade had no doubt her doing that might save his life at some point.

And they had never talked about her doing that. She had just offered to do it automatically.

They were already working as a team and he really liked that more than he wanted to admit.

And that got him thinking about other ways they could work together. He had to get used to the fact that he was the real world side and that she could see and do things he could never see or do.

He could actually arrest someone, but she could read the person's thoughts and find out intent and so much more.

After just one event on their first morning, he now felt even better and actually excited about working with Eve.

The rest of the morning was uneventful and they stopped for lunch at a Denny's Restaurant. Cascade kept his microphone on his head and she sat across from him so they could talk like a normal couple.

He liked that more than he wanted to admit, actually.

He ordered a French Dip and fries, which had sounded good to her as well, so when it came, she just took the ghost component of his meal. Before she took it, they did an experiment. He took a fry and tasted it, then she took the ghost components of everything and he tasted another fry.

The same taste. What she took didn't seem to bother at all what he was eating.

At lunch he told her how he had gone to college, had two degrees, then served four years in the Marines, seeing minor combat in the last stages of the Iraq war. Then he had gone through the police academy and discovered he was really, really good at everything to do with law enforcement.

At one point he asked her why she didn't actually know all of this already since she had been in his mind so much.

"Not surface," she had said. "And I respect your privacy so I never went digging.

And since he could be in her head when she was touching him, he did the same thing. So even though they knew each other's thoughts when touching, they were going to take time, like a regular couple, to learn all the deeper stuff.

And he liked that more than he wanted to admit.

"So is when you joined the force that you were recruited to be a superhero?" Eve asked.

He nodded, finishing off his last fry. "I still don't know much about this superhero business, but I'm learning."

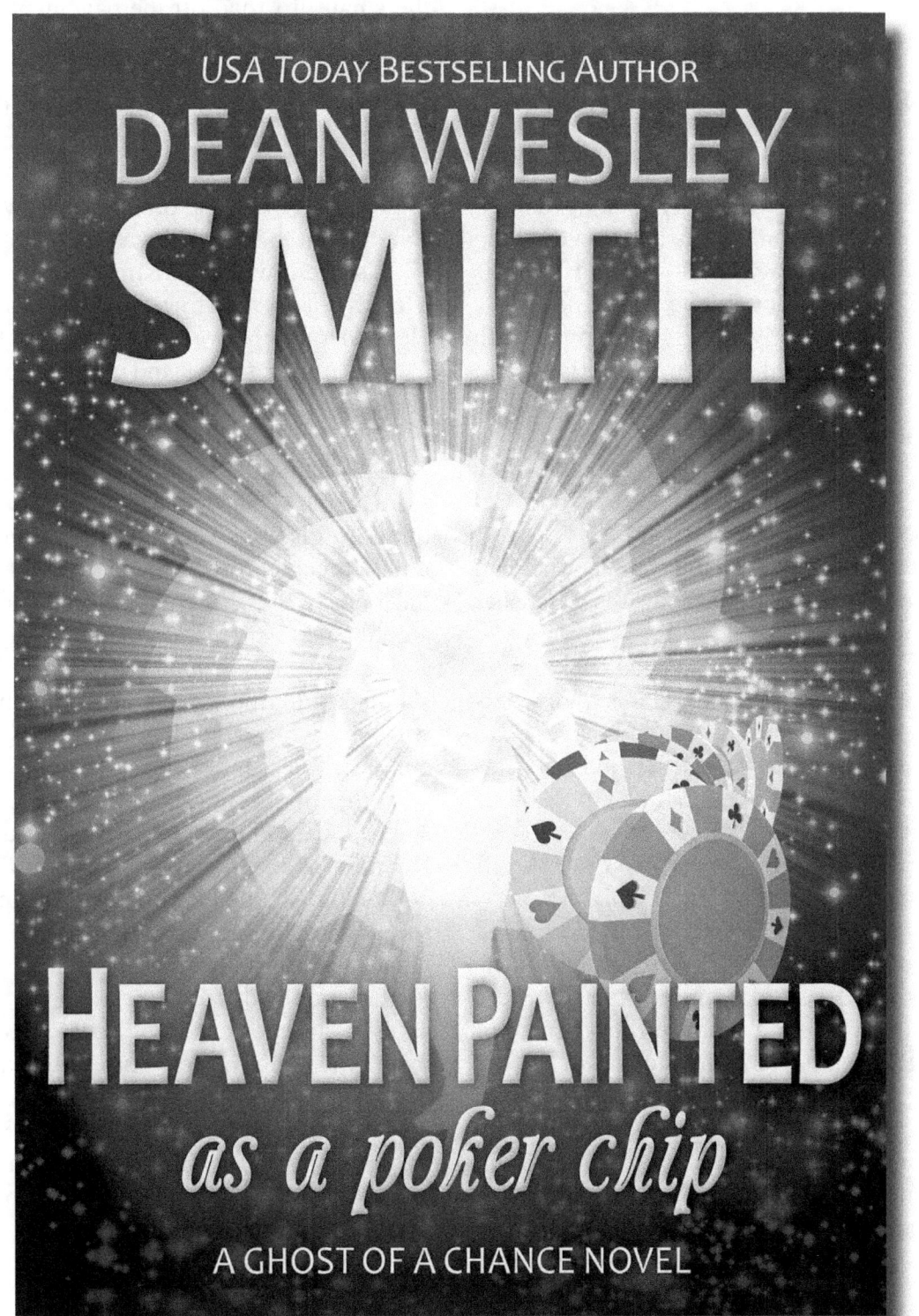

"So we can both learn together," she said, laughing.

"I like that idea a lot," he said.

And he did.

# TWELVE

**EVE REALLY HAD** enjoyed their lunch. She wanted to learn everything about Cascade without digging into his mind, even though she now knew how to do that easily. But for the time, with him, she would stay on the surface, and she knew he was doing the same with her when inside her head.

That showed that not only did they both care for each other, they both respected each other.

She couldn't remember if she had ever had a boyfriend who respected her in any fashion at all.

After lunch, they headed back out on patrol and thirty minutes later were working along a winding two-lane paved road that stayed next to a river and connected two of the smaller towns outside of Portland.

It seemed that Deputy Sheriff Cascade's territory to patrol was very, very large. The county was underfunded and thus the sheriff's department understaffed. Every day on patrol they were going to cover a lot of territory, much of it Eve had never seen before.

As they came around a corner, Eve spotting an old white panel van tucked up in the pine trees on her side. Something about it gave her a chill and she mentioned that to Cascade.

"Let's take a look," he said, frowning. "One thing I have been learning to trust is that gut-sense about things. Seems to come from somewhere."

He reported in where they were, what he was investigating, and then pulled up the small dirt road off the pavement and parked a distance behind the van.

The van was in a small clearing where the road turned around. Sun beat down on the panel van, but the trees around it looked dark and very uninviting.

Cascade started to run the plates while Eve got out to see what was happening.

As she did, a man came back down a trail out of the trees with a shovel. He had on bib overalls, a dirty white T-shirt under them, and heavy boots. He looked muddy, like he had been digging a while.

She had no idea really where they were at, but she had a hunch digging anything in this area was going to be illegal unless this guy owned the land, and from the looks of him, his greasy black hair and an old panel van, that seemed unlikely.

And as she saw him, every alarm bell she had in her head went off. Something was very wrong with him and it took her a moment to see it.

When in training the last few weeks, she had learned to look at people's auras. Her aura was extremely bright and full of colors, but she had it contained behind a shield because she was a ghost and even ghosts had enemies, she was told.

Cascade had a very, very bright aura as well, and her aura and his seemed to match in a lot of places. That had pleased her more than she wanted to admit, but so far had never told Cascade.

She had also learned that human auras often told a good story about who the person was.

This man's aura was black and very small.

He saw the sheriff's car and she could see him hesitate, clearly trying to calm himself and keep walking toward his van as if nothing was wrong.

"Time to see what you have been up to," Eve said.

She moved toward him and just let him walk right through her.

Evil.

Pure evil.

No wonder his aura was pure black. He didn't have a redeeming feature about him.

The guy had just buried a young girl he had killed, had another at his home in a basement, and was thinking about how he was now going to have to bury a cop as well. It didn't worry him, just annoyed him.

He had no guilt, no sense of anything but that he owned the world and could do what he pleased with other people's lives.

Eve let the man walk on, then she just bent over and threw up her lunch.

Never, in all her life, had she experienced anything like that. She had no idea that people like this man even existed on the planet.

As she tried to gather herself from the horrid thoughts of that piece of trash, behind her she heard Cascade open his car door and climb out.

Shit!

She had to do something. This guy had a large pistol stuck in his belt and was about to just gun down Cascade without a hesitation.

And Cascade was too far away to warn in any real way.

She turned and in three steps was back inside the blackness that was the guy she called human trash.

He had his hand on the revolver and was turned slightly toward his van to set down the shovel. He planned to set the shovel down, draw the revolver and kill Cascade.

But not on her watch.

Not on her first day.

Not today.

Not any damn day, actually.

She made him freeze like something had encased him in metal.

She could feel his panic start to rise as he tried to move.

"Nope, trash man. No moving for you."

The guy panicked even more hearing her voice.

Cascade must have seen her throw up, then turn and go back inside the guy. Cascade hadn't moved more than a step from his patrol car and he had his hand on his service pistol, but hadn't drawn it yet.

If she hadn't stopped this trash, Cascade would have never gotten that gun out in time to defend himself.

"Step away from the van!" Cascade shouted at the man.

The dashboard camera on the patrol car was operating, feeding a live stream back to headquarters, so she and Cascade were going to have to be careful how they handled this.

Eve decided she had had enough of the disgust in this guy's mind and with a simple tweak of a nerve that she had learned how to do in the last two weeks, she put the guy to sleep.

He fell to the ground and, as he did, his hand came out holding the large gun.

Eve stepped aside, trying to use the fresh afternoon air to clear her head. They had to save that girl at the guy's house. The girl was young and was in a metal box in his cellar. The trash had doubted she would be alive when he got back, since he planned on stopping for lunch along the way.

But the trash didn't care if the girl lived or died. He actually enjoyed playing with a dead girl's body at least until they started to smell and stiffen up.

That thought almost made Eve throw up again.

She glanced back at the piece of smelly trash slumped on the ground. He would be out for about ten minutes.

Cascade instantly had his gun out and was approaching the guy as he had been trained, calling for backup as he did.

"He buried a girl up in the trees beside a couple others he killed over the last year," Eve said.

Cascade nodded slightly, looking stunned.

"We got another girl in an airtight box in his basement," Eve said. "She isn't going to last much longer."

"Shit," Cascade said, softly.

Cascade got near the guy, kicked the guy over, shoved the gun aside, and then managed to get handcuffs on the guy.

Eve moved over to Cascade and touched him so they could talk inside his head.

"I can go into that trash again, wake him, get him to confess," she said.

"You can do that?" Cascade asked without speaking.

"Never done it, but been trained how and watched it a couple times," she said, showing Cascade her training. "If I get the trash to repent and tell us about the girl locked in his basement, we have a reason to get officers there quickly."

"Where is the trash's house?" Cascade asked without saying a word.

"Down off of I-5," she said. "Too far for us to make it in time to save her."

"Do it," Cascade said.

She let go of him and moved back to the piece of human garbage on the ground. Then she stepped into him again.

The blackness was intense, more than she had ever imagined it could be.

She got him to wake up and Cascade ordered the man to stay on his knees facing the patrol car and its camera.

Eve got the trash to do as Cascade ordered. Then she made the trash start bawling and sobbing like one of the girls he had killed.

"I don't want to do this anymore," the trash sobbed.

Then Eve, through the sobs, and loud enough for Cascade's microphone to pick up, got the trash to tell all about the women buried up the hill and how he wanted to save the girl in his basement.

Eve got the trash to tell Cascade his address and where the girl was exactly.

Then Eve had the guy say, "Hurry. I don't want another death on my conscience."

Eve knew this piece of human trash didn't have a conscience, but what the hell, it sounded good.

At that moment a second patrol car arrived, lights flashing, and another officer about Cascade's size and build, only with blond hair, scrambled up beside Cascade.

Eve got the trash to repeat what he had just said.

Cascade called it in, getting officers and medical personnel rushing to the man's house.

Eve decided that this man needed even more punishment.

Jewel, one of the other ghost agents who had been a doctor before she died, had shown her how to change a person's brain in a way that caused the person extreme pain at times.

Eve had never thought she would use that, so hadn't paid a lot of attention. But she wanted more than anything to use it now. So she needed help. This guy deserved that kind of punishment.

She tweaked the nerve again and the guy pitched forward flat onto his face in the dirt.

Eve stepped out and shouted into the air, "Jewel, need some help!"

Jewel had said to just call into the air when she needed help. And if Jewel could do what she said was possible, this was going to be fun.

# THIRTEEN

**CASCADE KNEW WITHOUT** reading Eve's thoughts that she had just saved his life.

That guy would have had that big gun up and firing before Cascade had a chance to even draw or duck for cover.

And the idea that he had come that close to death made him shake a little.

He had known something was wrong when Eve had left the guy and thrown up. He should have reacted differently right then. But that would come with more time together.

This was still only their first day. They needed to learn a lot more about each other.

Then when Eve had shown him what was in the guy's head and what he had done and about the girl in the basement about to die, Cascade had wanted to throw up as well.

Then Eve did something he couldn't imagine doing. She offered to go back inside an evil man's head and make him confess to try to save the girl.

Eve was a lot, lot stronger than even she thought she was. Wow.

She got the guy to wake up and get on his knees, facing the camera on the patrol car and speaking loud enough to be picked up by Cascade's microphone. Then the guy confessed twice, once to Cascade and a second time as Jimmy, another sheriff's deputy, arrived on scene.

Cascade got emergency police headed to the guy's home with an ambulance.

Then, as he was finished, Eve put the guy to sleep again and stepped out of the evil.

Then she did something that Cascade hadn't expected.

She called for another ghost agent. The one that had trained Eve over the last month or so.

Was something more happening?

What was wrong?

A woman appeared who seemed to be about Eve's age. The woman, who Cascade assumed was Jewel because that was who Eve had called for, was wearing a thin tan bikini under an open shimmering robe. And she could wear that bikini.

Her hair was pulled back and she had suntan lotion on that smelled slightly of coconut butter.

The woman nodded at Cascade who kept a pose as if he couldn't see a woman in a skimpy bikini standing near a murderer in the pine trees in Oregon.

"Looks like the problem is pretty well covered here," Jewel said, taking a glance at the man on the ground. She turned to Eve. "So why the call?"

"Piece of trash there killed a bunch of women," Eve said, "just buried one up in the trees here, and has another he planned to play with when he got home, dead or alive, locked in a metal box in his basement."

"Shit," Jewel said, shaking her head and then looking with disgust at the man sprawled on the ground.

Then she smiled and turned back to Eve. "Now I understand. You think this guy deserves a little more punishment than this fine, handsome policeman can give him?"

"I do," Eve said, winking at Cascade. "And I know you showed me how, but damned if I trust myself enough on my first day to try it."

"Come with me," Jewel said, taking Eve's hand.

And as Cascade watched, his ghost partner and a woman in a bikini vanished inside the body of an evil killer.

Just vanished.

# FOURTEEN

**EVE DIDN'T WANT** to go back inside the piece of trash, but with Jewel with her, it felt better.

Hand-in-hand, they both went into the evil blackness that was the piece of trash's mind.

"Oh, one of the worst I have seen," Jewel said to Eve.

Eve could feel Jewel actually shudder.

"I hope to not see another this bad in a lot of years," Eve said.

"They are out there, sadly," Jewel said. "That's why we have the jobs we do."

Then, in the back of the man's brain, Jewel once again took Eve step-by-step through the process of how to make certain thoughts generate extreme pain.

It seems that Jewel had been a medical doctor before being killed and becoming a ghost agent. And that medical training came in handy a lot.

Together, Eve and Jewel set the thoughts that would cause this trash pile of a human being pain. Since he hadn't cared about the pain of his victims, it seemed like a fair justice to have him now feel some of that pain.

They left the trash, still hand-in-hand, laughing.

Cascade watched them appear, one eyebrow up in question.

Two other cop cars had just arrived.

"We just gave this trash something to think about is all," Eve said to Cascade.

"I think you'll find it amusing," Jewel said to Cascade. "And nice meeting you. Take care of our new recruit."

He nodded and Jewel vanished.

At that moment, the piece of trash on the ground started to moan and try to struggle back to his knees.

The third cop coming up to the group said, "Great job, Cascade. They got the girl out of the box in this guy's basement and she's alive and on her way to the hospital."

Eve applauded and Cascade smiled.

"Read him his rights," Eve said, "And I'll get him to confess again."

Cascade put his gun away, got out the rights card in his shirt pocket and started reading the trash his rights as if he was a real human being.

Eve went back inside the dark, evil brain one more time and got the guy to cry slightly again.

"Do you understand your rights?" Cascade asked the trash.

"I do," she got the guy to say.

That was on the dash camera and an officer cam one officer was wearing.

"Would you like to tell us what you were doing up that hill there?" Cascade asked.

She got the trash, through tears and sobs to make it believable, explain how he buried another body up there and where everyone he had killed was buried. And then she got him to confess to kidnapping and putting the girl in the box in his basement with the intent of killing her and having sex with her dead body.

"You are one sick piece of trash," the blond cop said as Eve left the guy.

The two new cops on the scene moved to pull the guy up from his knees.

"Ask him if he enjoyed making love to the girls," Eve said to Cascade, smiling.

Cascade did and the piece of trash started to smile. Then the trash got this horrid look and screamed in agony and went to the ground, peeing himself as he did.

"Oh, great," one of the cops said.

The two cops yanked him back to his feet and started to drag him toward their cars.

The trash just kept screaming.

Eve went over to Cascade and put her hand on his shoulder.

"What did you and that other ghost Jewel do to the human trash?" Cascade asked without saying anything out loud.

"We just rewired his brain a slight bit is all," Eve said, laughing. "Now when he thinks about sex with anyone, boy or girl, young or old, it will feel like someone has kicked him in the groin really hard."

"You didn't?" he thought at her, but she could tell it was everything he could do to not burst out laughing.

"Other ghosts have done this to perverts and killers like this one," Eve told him. "So many times in fact, the problem

is starting to get known in the medical community."

"I think I love this job," Cascade said.

"As soon as those guy's memories fade from my mind," Eve said, "I will as well."

## FIFTEEN

**"MEMORIES ALMOST FADED?"** Cascade asked her as the two of them sat in his living room, facing each other, sipping on a wonderful white wine. He had cooked them both a fantastic dinner of stuffed sage hen and steamed vegetables. Best meal she remembered tasting in a long time.

She said she felt bad that she couldn't cook for him but he could cook for her, since she could eat the ghost part of his meal. That was when she discovered that he loved to cook, had thought of being a chef instead of a cop after the Marines. So the fact that he could cook something for himself and have two people enjoy it was wonderful to him.

This handsome superhero really was too good to be true.

"Memories from the trash are gone," she said, smiling at him. "One of the nice things about being a ghost, the memories of people we brush through or are inside of don't stick with us for very long."

He raised his glass. "To a good first day, partner. Thanks for saving my life."

"I think that's what partners are for," she said.

After that they watched a movie and both of them fell asleep on the couch together, her inside him.

It felt wonderful to sleep with him like that.

Natural.

He woke up first and stirred her and she agreed she would see him bright and early in the morning for their second day.

He wanted her to stay and she wanted to stay. But they would have time to talk about that soon enough.

Days of time riding around in a patrol car, actually.

She jumped to her condo, which actually felt empty.

She should be staying with him, making love to him.

Or at least sleeping in his arms as they had done on the couch.

She was a ghost, he was a superhero. Somehow, someone, somewhere, would know what she and Cascade could do to take the relationship to the next level.

They both wanted to.

She took a quick shower, then crawled into her wonderful bed, thinking about him.

He was handsome and he could cook and he liked her.

And today they had saved a life and helped a child be born safely.

Pretty damn fine first day together.

She fell asleep thinking of his wonderful smile.

And she was pretty sure she had a smile on her face as well.

## PART THREE
*Saving More Lives*

## SIXTEEN

**HOW CAN A** ghost make love to a live superhero?

That was the problem that Eve and Cascade had been trying to figure out for their first full month as a team. So far, without success.

But even with that minor problem, the first month had been fantastic as far as Cascade was concerned.

They shared everything else.

So everyday he was on duty, Eve rode with him. And she saw things that at times he missed. She could see a person's aura and from what he had seen through her thoughts, a bad person's aura was mostly black.

So not only did they go looking for speeders and do their standard patrols, but they also went looking for black auras.

And in their first month they had found a couple.

The first had been on their first day with the killer, but the second major black aura on a person had been during their third week together.

They had just finished with lunch at a nice dinner called Mary's beside the large mall near Tigard, Oregon. They were walking back toward the patrol car when Eve touched his arm and had him stop.

He could sense she was alarmed.

"Look through my eyes," she said.

They had practiced that a few times and it always felt weird.

He turned with her and mostly closed his own eyes because otherwise he would be seeing through his own eyes and hers and that had made him dizzy almost every time.

What she was seeing was a man in jeans, a long duster-like coat buttoned up even though it was almost ninety degrees, and tennis shoes. He had a shaved head and sunglasses covering his eyes.

"Look at his aura," Eve said.

"Black," he said.

"Sickly black," Eve said as Cascade opened his own eyes and looked at the man walking along the edge of the mall toward an entrance.

Every alarm in his head was going off.

"Jewel told me when someone had a sickly black aura, they were about to commit something truly evil."

"Let's go!" Cascade said.

He was carrying a portable mike and reported in at once where he was at, what he had seen, and that he needed backup at once.

"I'm going to see if I can catch him and find out what's going on," Eve said.

At a run, she headed for him just as he reached the mall entrance.

It was then, with Eve still a good fifty yards from the man, that the guy opened up his trench coat and pulled out what looked to be some form of automatic rifle. It was nothing like a gun that Cascade had seen before.

Clearly something Russian or Chinese and it had a very large magazine inserted in it.

That gun was made for killing.

On a run toward the man, Cascade called in an update and then had his gun out.

At that point a few people started screaming and running away from the man.

Eve went right through a couple of the people and then saw the man had the gun out and was lifting it.

She instantly jumped to beside him.

And then vanished inside the guy.

The guy froze and dropped the gun.

Eve had just saved a lot of lives.

# SEVENTEEN

**EVE HATED BEING** inside of sick humans.

And this guy named Calvin was as sick as they came. He just wanted to kill people and had actually been looking forward to killing a lot of people in the mall and then some police.

Calvin was young, not more than twenty. A high-school dropout and a person his parents and family had disowned.

Calvin was going to show them he could amount to something.

He knew if he did a lot of killing, the press would make him famous because that's what they did. If you killed enough people, you got famous.

And he wanted to be famous.

He wanted his parents to know he was famous.

He knew that people should worship him and follow him and he needed the press and everyone to know he could carry through and earn their respect by killing.

Eve was disgusted at the very belief.

She froze him down solid and got him to drop his gun.

Then she was about to tweak his nerve to put him asleep when she realized he had a friend.

A friend as sick as he was.

Lewis.

Same age.

Same sickness.

Lewis wanted to be famous as well.

Their plan was for Calvin to go into the mall first, start killing people, get the people stampeding toward the other side of the mall and Lewis would kill them as they ran toward him.

Eve snapped the nerve on Calvin and he dropped the floor, out like a light just as Cascade reached them.

"He's got a friend on the other side of the mall," Eve said. "Get help there quick. I'll see if I can stop him in time."

Cascade nodded and was calling in instructions again.

Eve instantly jumped to the other side of the mall.

Lewis also had on a long coat and still had it buttoned. And he was looking puzzled because people were moving toward him, but there had been no shots fired.

Eve merged inside of him.

This kid was as sick as his friend. And was excited about killing and becoming famous.

"Not today, asshole," Eve said to the sick brain.

She had the kid open his coat and then put his hands over his head. Then she had him lean back against the wall so the police that had just pulled up outside would see him.

Then she had an idea.

A nasty idea, but an idea.

She went back to the part of the kid's brain where Jewel had shown her with the girl killer a few weeks back. And there she set a command and rewired his brain just a little bit.

At that point the police got there.

Five of them approached and got the kid's gun and got him on the ground.

Then she left him, standing off to one side to watch.

He wanted to be famous. Well, he was going to be famous for crying his eyes out anytime his name was mentioned.

For the moment, the kid looked defiant and smiling. People were taking pictures of him on their cell phones.

"What's your name?" one of the cops asked.

The kid started to say Lewis and burst into tears and collapsed on the ground.

Eve looked around at all the people filming the gunman crying like a baby and laughed.

She jumped back to Cascade. He and three other cops had the unconscious Calvin handcuffed and on his stomach on the ground.

She touched Cascade's arm. "Got the other one."

"Great," Cascade said in his inner voice. "Are we done?"

"Don't know," Eve said. She had a feeling she had missed something.

So she said, "I'm going back into this guy to see if there's anything we missed."

"Good idea," Cascade said, again in his inner voice.

Eve crawled inside the guy and got him to wake up some.

He had no idea why his plan hadn't worked. But then she saw that he had a second plan.

And his second plan would kill even more than he would have killed here in the mall today.

They had two cars loaded with explosives from his grandfather's factory. He had driven one and Lewis had driven the other.

The bombs would level both sides of the mall and both parking lots on the sides of the mall away from where he and Lewis had entered.

And they were set to go off in exactly twenty-six minutes. Just as the police were emptying the mall.

Eve quickly rewired this idiot's brain as well to make him proclaim his plan over and over and over anytime anyone asked him any kind of question. And to proclaim his superiority over everyone else as well.

## Some Classic Dean Wesley Smith Stories
### Available at your favorite booksellers.

And she also had him tell anyone who was listening how to defuse the bombs he had built.

And he would do that over and over for the rest of his life.

He was not going to be popular in prison.

And he would deserve everything he got there, if he lived to get that far.

# EIGHTEEN

**CASCADE WATCHED** as Eve appeared out of the gunman and moved over beside him.

Two cops had the gunman pinned and were about to bring him to his feet.

"Both of their cars are rigged with massive amounts of explosives to go off in just over twenty minutes."

"Shit," Cascade said in his inner voice.

"Their cars are parked at the other two main entrances," Eve said, touching Cascade and showing him what she knew about defusing the bombs.

Cascade nodded.

"Ask him to tell you how to defuse the bombs," Eve said.

Cascade nodded and stepped toward Calvin.

"Any more of you idiots beside you and your partner on the other side of the mall?" Cascade demanded. "Anything else like bombs in your cars?"

Calvin smiled and then got a frown as he started telling Cascade all about the bombs and his great plan to kill even more people."

Cascade felt disgusted. He could only imagine how Eve felt crawling around inside the guy's head.

"How do we disarm them?" Cascade demanded.

Calvin was frowning, but he rattled off how exactly to disarm them, how to go in the passenger door and the detonator was on the floor of the passenger seat.

There were now five cops there.

Cascade asked what both cars looked like and Calvin told them, proclaiming how smart he was and how many people were going to die.

"Can we trust him?" Officer Daniels of the Tigard Department asked.

Cascade knew him as a good guy and really smart and a cop who often ran in when calling for help might have been a better solution.

"I think we can," Cascade said, nodding. "Get the bomb squad on the way and close off those entrances and get people leaving the mall through this and the entrance with the other gunman. I'll take the car on the west side."

Daniels nodded. "I'll take the east side."

At that Cascade turned and went around the mall toward the west at full run while Daniels went the other way.

As he came around the corner he saw Eve pointing at the car he needed to find.

He shouted for a couple of people near other cars to run and they did.

"Sure wish I could teleport like you do," he said to Eve as he got to the car winded.

"More than likely you can," Eve said. "Other superheroes can. You just haven't learned how yet. So if this bomb starts to go, you just think you want to be back by the patrol car real hard."

"Is that possible?" he asked as he stared in at the massive explosives filling the back seat of the car.

# Now Available
## from all your favorite booksellers
## in trade paper and electronic editions.

"Believe it is," Eve said. "I have no intention of losing a partner this soon in our relationship.

He nodded.

With that, he took a deep breath and opened the passenger door.

And nothing exploded.

So far, so good.

## NINETEEN

**EVE WATCHED** as Cascade followed the guy's instructions perfectly, leaning over the passenger seat and working with the detonator on the floor.

Within one minute he had the bomb defused.

He stood and stepped back.

She touched him.

On the outside he seemed cool and collected, but he was waves of relief inside.

She said to him that she wished she could kiss him for that great work.

"Thanks," he said. "Think you can help Daniels?"

"I can if you move away from this car," she said.

"Gladly," he said, moving back and waving even more people out of the area.

She jumped to the other side of the mall.

Daniels had the passenger door of the other car open, but seemed to be having issues with something. He was just staring at the detonator.

She merged with him.

As Cascade had thought, Daniels was a good guy, living with a life partner who worked for Intel. They were considering trying to adopt.

And he loved being a cop. He loved helping people.

But he was having trouble remembering exactly which way to go. He had started to doubt himself and was about to back out and let the car explode.

She carefully fed him some confidence and the correct instructions in such a way that he wouldn't realize he got it from anything but himself.

He nodded, took a deep breath and went back to work on the bomb.

Eve stayed with him, keeping him completely focused and sure of the instructions.

And with eight minutes to spare, he had the bomb disarmed.

Then she planted the thought, "Just to be sure, back the hell out of here and clear the area."

He did just that and as he left the car, she turned and left him.

He did exactly what Cascade was doing on the other side of the mall. He waved people away, then headed for the mall doors to get people away from the big glass doors and back down the hallway.

If that thing blew after all, it wouldn't kill anyone, but it was going to make an awful mess.

She jumped back to Cascade and smiled at him. "He's got it."

Cascade smiled, then said to everyone in the mall close to the doors. "Everyone down or take cover," he said. "Just in case."

Nothing exploded.

As far as Eve was concerned, tonight they were having a great dinner and wine and she just might do whatever she could to have sex with the handsome man who had saved a lot of lives today.

Of course, it didn't work. He was a human and she was a ghost.

But it was still a wonderful dinner.

## PART FOUR
*They Don't Want to Sleep*

## TWENTY

**FOR A GHOST** and a superhero, what exactly was the next level?

He could see her just fine, but they couldn't really touch each other. Granted, being in each other's minds was pretty damn nifty as far as she was concerned, but they were both very, very horny.

So far they had managed to avoid it because they had no answer to how to have a physical relationship. But Eve knew they had to solve this very, very frustrating problem.

And fast.

So on Saturday afternoon, Eve decided to go try to get some answers.

Cascade was stretched out in front of the television by 9 in the morning in his apartment, and she had no doubt he would be asleep in ten minutes. Having a ghost in his head all the time was tiring. He hadn't been a superhero much longer than she had been a ghost, so all this was new for both of them.

She was tired as well.

But the sex thing needed to get solved.

She had set up a meeting with Jewel and her boyfriend, Tommy, at their normal breakfast place, the Golden Nugget Buffet in Las Vegas. So with an air kiss to her partner, she jumped from outside Portland, Oregon, to Vegas.

Tommy had been a cop when alive and Jewel a doctor. They were the two Ghost of a Chance agents that had trained her in what she could do as an agent in this new life, and she had called Jewel a couple of times the first month for different forms of help.

This morning, Jewel had on a beautiful blue blouse and had her long brown hair pulled back off her face. Tommy had on a T-shirt with a light shirt over it. With his close-cut brown hair, he reminded Eve a lot of Cascade.

Both Jewel and Tommy were tall and exercised every day a great deal, mostly running.

Jewel and Tommy had both died in a car wreck as she had done. They had just met and as a deputy, he was driving Jewel, as a doctor, to an emergency in the Montana mountains when a deer jumped in front of them and they had hit a tree.

As had happened to Eve, instead of crossing over, Jewel had remained in this real world and been recruited as a Ghost of a Chance agent. Jewel and Tommy had been recruited as agents together and had fallen in love.

Eve liked Jewel and Tommy a great deal and felt as if she could trust them with anything.

They had already finished their breakfast and were sipping on coffee when she arrived.

In one month, eating had become one of her real pleasures in being dead, besides being with Cascade. And being able to read other people's thoughts and walk though things. That was all fun as well, but mostly she just loved every minute with Cascade.

Jewel and Tommy were much later morning people than she and Cascade were, because of his job schedule. Jewel and Tommy had just finished breakfast, for her it was getting closer to lunch.

The Golden Nugget had a wonderful feel about it. Brown cloth decorations, brown oak wood, and large windows looking out over the pool gave the place a feeling of relaxation instead of Las Vegas hurry-up-and-spend of so many of the casinos.

There were only about twenty live humans scattered around the large room and Jewel and Tommy had a table off to one side near a planter. It seemed that they always had that table. Live humans never sat there.

When Eve had trained here in Vegas after her death, she and Jewel and Tommy had spent a lot of time right here in this buffet at the same table.

The smell of bacon and waffles filled the air and even though she had eaten a few hours before, she went for a waffle as dessert. Damn she was loving to eat, but Jewel had warned Eve that she had better get exercising fairly quickly. It seemed that ghosts could gain weight, and with as good as food tasted, Eve could see how it wouldn't be hard to stack on the pounds.

Eve joined Jewel and Tommy and they asked about her and Cascade's first month and she filled them in as she worked on her waffle.

"I sometimes miss just riding on patrol," Tommy said. "It was always a combination of quiet boredom combined at times with acute awareness and broken by moments of panicked action."

"Would you leave this life for that again?" Jewel asked him.

He laughed. "Not a chance."

All three of them laughed, then Jewel focused on Eve. "So what's the problem?"

Eve took a deep breath, trying to figure out where to start. Then she decided to just tell them what was happening instead of asking questions around the problem.

"Cascade and I have fallen in love," she said.

"Wow, that's wonderful to hear," Jewel said, smiling a huge grin.

"It will sure make spending all those hours together a lot more fun," Tommy said, also smiling.

"It is fun," Eve said. "More than either of us have ever experienced before. We are sharing things I didn't know I would ever share with anyone else. And he's just an amazingly special person."

"So what's the problem?" Jewel asked.

Tommy laughed and looked at his partner, shaking his head at Jewel. "Sex."

"Oh," Jewel said, suddenly sitting back as she realized Eve's problem.

"Yeah," Eve said. "The problem, put bluntly, is that Cascade and I are beyond horny and damned if we can figure out the ghost-and-alive-connection problem."

"Oh," Jewel said again.

Eve pushed the remains of her waffle away. From Jewel's reaction, this was not going to be an easy problem to solve.

If there was a solution at all.

# TWENTY-ONE

**"WE NEED SOME** help with this one," Jewel said.

Tommy nodded.

And before Eve could stop Jewel or even ask who the help might be, Jewel said into the air, "K.J., a little help."

"Need a minute to finishing getting dressed if you don't mind." A voice in the air above the table seemed to echo from a deep chamber.

Eve looked around, but, of course, no one was there.

Jewel turned to Eve. "K.J. is our team's boss. He is the one who reports to the gods and he is the one who gets us our assignments, unlike you and Cascade who just go out and save people."

"Good thinking," Tommy said to Jewel. "K.J. has been dead for over a hundred years and has a reputation as a party person."

"One of the best, if not the best party person," a man said, appearing next to the table. "Please, if you must spread my reputation, do it with some accuracy."

The guy was short, really, really short, wearing a gray pinstriped silk suit and vest, a pink tie with flamingos on it, pink slippers, and a bright pink feathery hat that had a tail on it that went down his back.

Eve just stared, her mouth open. Her life in Oregon had been sheltered, clearly.

He bowed slightly to Eve, the feathers in his hat flowing around him. "I am K.J. I have heard you are a fast study."

"I had good instructors," Eve managed to say, nodding to Tommy and Jewel.

K.J. glanced at the buffet, then looked at Jewel. "Before I move to get some maple syrup on this grand tie, what is your problem?"

Jewel indicated that K.J. should sit down at the table.

"A major issue I see," K.J. said, sitting.

"You have heard," Jewel said, "that Eve is the first ghost agent to partner with a live superhero."

"How is that going?" K.J. said. "A grand experiment, if I must say."

"We are doing well," Eve said. "Saved a bunch of lives so far."

"And that is why we are here in this ghostly state," K.J. said, nodding.

"But Eve and her partner, Deputy McCall Cascade, have a problem," Jewel said.

"You are with Cascade?" K.J. said, his eyes lighting up.

Eve was surprised, because in all the times inside of Cascade's head, she had never seen a thought about this sparklingly-dressed ghost. She was sure she would have remembered. And positive Cascade would have remembered K.J. as well.

"I am," she said.

"Oh, girl, how do you keep your hands off of that hunk of a man?" K.J. asked. "I saw his picture when he was re-

cruited and got so hot I had to retire for the day and take care of issues."

Eve was fairly certain her face was bright red.

Jewel and Tommy were both laughing.

"That's the problem we called you here about," Jewel finally said.

"I can see no problem at all with climbing all over that hunk of a man," K.J. said. He looked at Eve. "Is it dreamy to be riding with him in his masculine patrol car with all the leather seats and the wonderful tools of manhood?"

She blushed again and laughed. "It is dreamy, yes."

"I knew it would be," K.J. said, clapping his hands. "Just knew it. You are one lucky ghost, girl."

"I think so," Eve said.

"So," Jewel said, between laughter. "How do they go about having sex?"

K.J. looked at Jewel, then back to Eve with a sly grin on his face.

"Oh, girl you are a fast mover, aren't you?"

## TWENTY-TWO

**EVE FIGURED HER** face was about as red as it was going to get, so she smiled at K.J. Then said, "Do you blame me?"

"Oh, my, not at all," K.J. said, fanning himself.

Eve thought Tommy was going to fall out of his chair laughing.

Jewel was trying to hold it together enough to actually get an answer out of K.J.

Eve was really starting to like this crazy ghost of a boss.

"So, what is needed," Jewel asked, "for these two to have sex? Real sex."

"Passion," K.J. said, "but with that hunk of a man, I doubt that is your problem, is it?"

"It is not," Eve said, smiling at him. "And it is not his problem toward me either. We both want this, but both of us are so new to our worlds, we have no idea how to go about that part of a relationship."

"Like two teenagers in the backseat of a car," K.J. said. "The fumbling is half the fun I am told."

"All I remember is the fear and the worry and the sweating," Jewel said.

Again, Tommy just laughed and shook his head.

Eve hadn't had any experience in back seats of cars. And her first sexual experiences hadn't been that rewarding, actually. And her sexual experiences with her loser of a husband hadn't changed that. So with Cascade, she was hoping for a little more.

Actually, a lot more.

K.J. looked at her. "You ever read the fine short story 'Man of Steel, Woman of Kleenex'?"

Eve shook her head. She had no idea what he was talking about.

Again Tommy laughed and Jewel just looked at K.J. with a stern look.

"No?" K.J. asked Eve. "For the better, since even though Cascade is a superhero and someone can put a hand through you like Kleenex, the situation in the story does not apply."

Tommy had to catch himself from laughing himself off his chair. If they hadn't been ghosts, everyone in the place would have been staring at them.

"K.J.," Jewel said, pretending to put on a stern face. "This is a serious problem that these two young lovers are trying to solve."

K.J. was laughing with Tommy at his own joke, but finally nodded and took a moment to catch his breath.

Eve was going to have to look up that story just to see why they were laughing.

Finally K.J. looked at both Jewel and Tommy. "I will teach you all a very nifty trick that none of your team knows yet, but that might come in handy at times."

He glanced around, clearly to make sure none of the live customers were watching, even though none of the four of them could be seen. Then K.J. reached forward and picked up the Keno ticket holder in the center of the table.

Not just the ghost element of the ticket holder, but the entire holder.

Then he set it down on the table with an audible click, smiling.

"Damn," Tommy said. "How did you do that?"

K.J. pointed to his head. "Just as we do all of our skills. I just imagined it."

"So we can cross over into the real world without controlling a person to do it for us?" Jewel asked, clearly as stunned as Eve was feeling.

"Within limits," K.J. said. "As far as I know, a normal human can't see us no matter what we do. Something about light and things I didn't understand."

"Cascade can see me fine thanks to Reanna," Eve said.

"Makes sense because he's a superhero," K.J. said, nodding.

K.J. then stood and indicated all three of them should follow him over to a planter filled with artificial plants that divided the buffet from a small lobby at the top of an escalator.

"Put your hand through the plants," K.J. said to each of them.

They all did.

Eve had gotten used to walking through things and not feeling a thing. She actually kind of liked it.

"Now," K.J. said, "Imagine your hand is solid enough to move a plant leaf."

Eve used what Jewel and Tommy had taught her about imagining being in different places and just being there, and floating, and so on. All of her training had been on using her imagination. It seemed that ghosts felt like they were part of this world, but were not really, so then had what seemed like powers to jump anywhere they could imagine or float places, or make others do as a ghost wanted.

Ghosts felt like they were tied to this world, but actually were not, thus their imagination had to break them free.

Eve focused that same imagination energy on making her hand solid and touching the plant leaf.

And suddenly she could feel the leaf. Not the ghost element of the leaf, that had a certain feel, but the actual artificial leaf.

It moved under her touch.

Jewel and Tommy had the same success.

"Wonderful! K.J. said, clapping his hands like a teenager happy to see someone.

He turned and went back to the table. As he did, Eve watched him study the room to make sure no one was looking, then he pulled out a chair that was tucked in too close to the table.

Not the ghost part of the chair, but the actual chair.

To any live person watching, either in the restaurant or on a camera, that chair must have looked like it had moved by itself.

Jewel, Tommy, and Eve tried to move a chair, but even though they all could feel the chair's surface, they couldn't get enough grip or energy to move it.

"This takes time and practice to learn," K.J. said as they all sat back down.

Then he turned to Eve. "But I have discovered over the years, after many pleasurable nights in my oversized hot tub with wonderful and very-much-alive superheroes who could see me, the practice is very much worth the effort."

Eve was again convinced she was blushing.

"That's how you and Madge from the diner did it," Tommy said, smiling.

Eve figured he was clearly talking about an event before she had died. She would ask later.

"A fella doesn't kiss and tell," K.J. said, laughing.

Jewel just laughed and shook her head.

"If I can make my hand solid to touch something," Eve asked, "can I make other parts of my body solid as well for Cascade's touch?"

K.J. smiled and fanned himself again with an imaginary fan. "With practice, Mr. Hunk Cascade can feel any part of you that you would want him to feel."

Eve was about to jump up and down for joy.

She smiled at Jewel and Tommy. "Thank you both."

Then she stood and moved over and kissed K.J. solidly on the cheek.

"And thank you," Eve said to K.J. "And now I need to go do some practicing on Cascade's wonderful and very masculine body."

"I think I might have the vapors just thinking of that," K.J. said, again fanning himself.

She laughed and jumped back to Cascade's apartment.

He was stretched out on the couch, sound asleep. She knelt by the couch and then gently touched his face.

The light stubble on his cheeks felt wonderful against her hand.

He stirred as she brushed his cheek again. He smiled and opened his eyes.

"That felt wonderful," he said, looking into her eyes.

"It did," she said.

"How?" he asked.

"I'll explain it all later," she said.

Then she stood and stripped off her clothes as he watched intently. Quickly she was standing in front of him completely naked and enjoying his look.

All he could do was stare.

Finally he said, "You are so beautiful."

She imagined her hand firm and reached out for his hand.

"Come on," she said, actually feeling his hand solidly in hers as she pulled him to his feet. "We have some practicing to do."

"What kind of practicing?" he asked, smiling.

"The best kind," she said. "The very best."

And with that, Eve was convinced after just an hour of practice that they would live happily ever after together.

Only one small problem.

She was dead.

But it seemed that was a problem they could now live with.

---

# Now Available
## from all your favorite booksellers
## in trade paper and electronic editions.

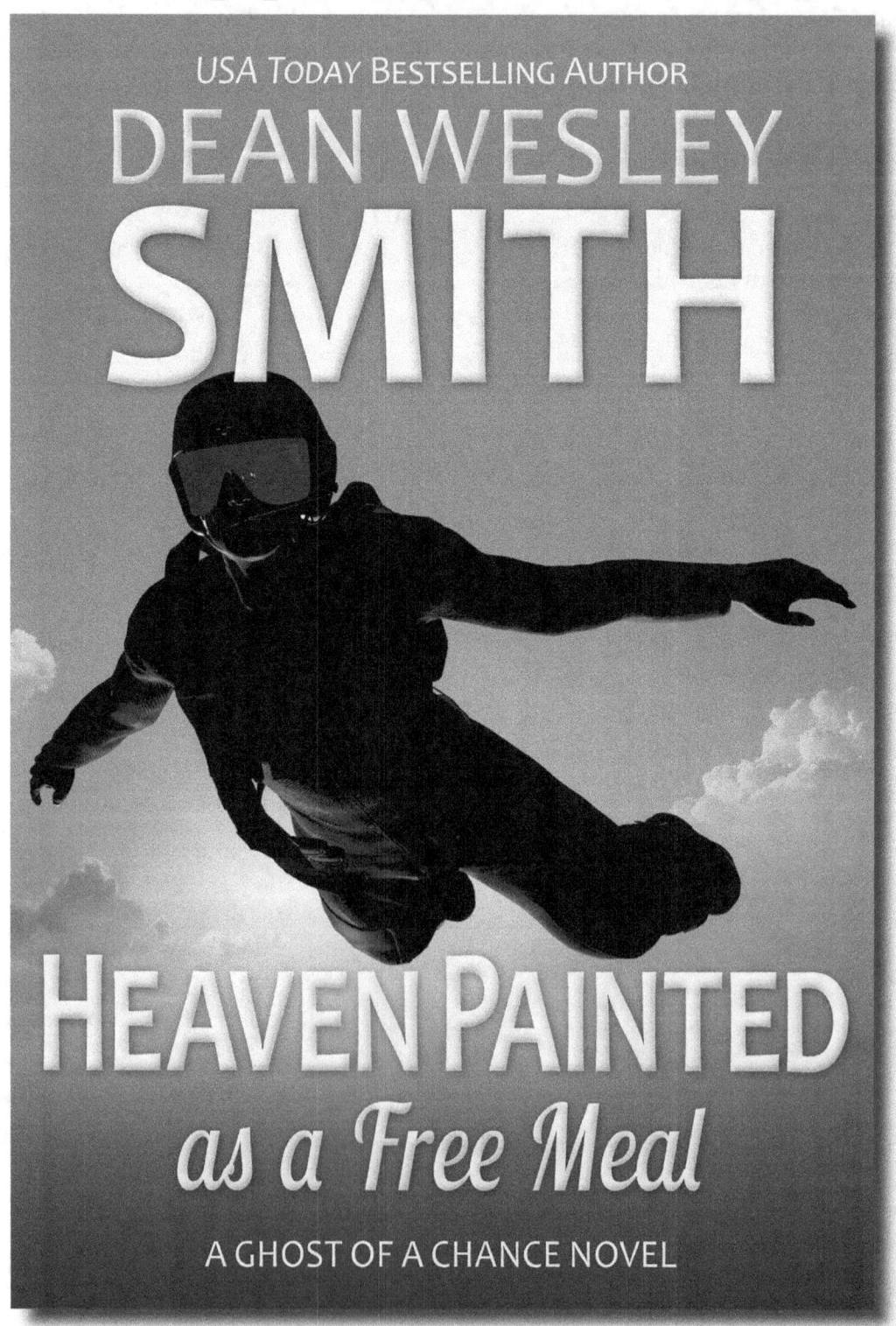

# Now Available
## from all your favorite booksellers in trade paper and electronic editions.

USA TODAY BESTSELLING AUTHOR

# DEAN WESLEY SMITH

## HEAVEN PAINTED
### as a Christmas Gift

A GHOST OF A CHANCE NOVEL

**#1... October 2013**

**#2... November 2013**

**#3... December 2013**

**#4... January 2014**

**#5... February 2014**

**#6... March 2014**

**#7... April 2014**

**#8... May 2014**

**#9... June 2014**

**HEAVEN PAINTED AS A POKER CHIP**
*A Full Novel in the Ghost of a Chance series*

*#10... July 2014*

**THE HIGH EDGE**
*A Seeders Universe Novel*

*#11... August 2014*

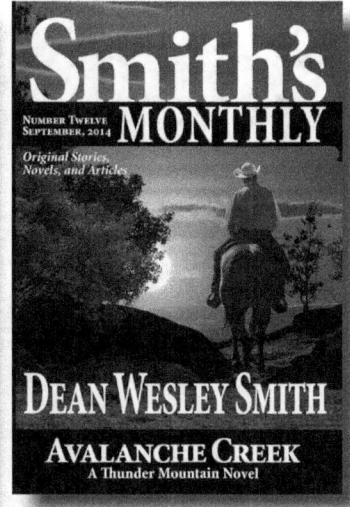
**AVALANCHE CREEK**
*A Thunder Mountain Novel*

*#12...September 2014*

**HEAVEN PAINTED AS A CHRISTMAS GIFT**
*A Ghost of a Chance Novel*

*#13...October 2014*

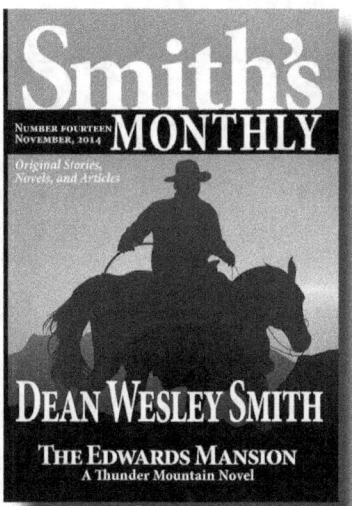
**THE EDWARDS MANSION**
*A Thunder Mountain Novel*

*#14...November 2014*

**COLD CALL**
*A Cold Poker Gang Novel*

*#15...December 2014*

**LAKE ROOSEVELT**
*A Thunder Mountain Novel*

*#16...January 2015*

**WARM SPRINGS**
*A Thunder Mountain Novel*

*#17...February 2015*

**CALLING DEAD**
*A Cold Poker Gang Novel*

*#18...March 2015*

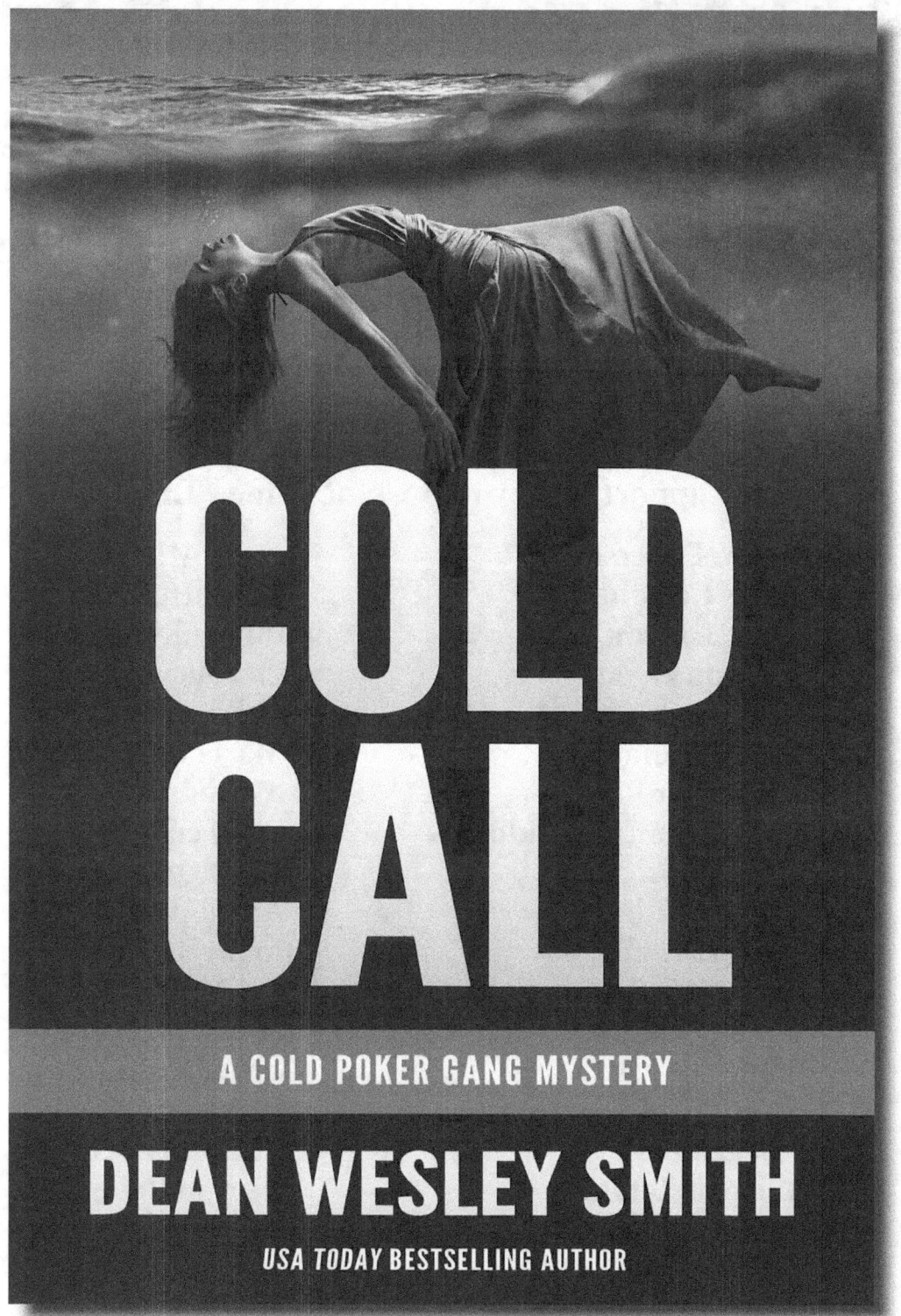

# Thank You!!

I would like to thank the following wonderful people who support my blog and my work through Patreon. Your support is very important to me.  Thanks!

| | |
|---|---|
| Irette Y. Patterson | Terry Mixon |
| Chris Cousino | James Husun |
| Jane Lawson | Kathryn Rooney |
| Shantnu Tiwari | Sherman Cox |
| Rob Cornell | Chong Go |
| Erick Lindman | Maria Grace |
| Christopher Ridge | Grondpom |
| Miguel Angel Alonso Pulido | Fen |
| Nancy Hendrickson | Livia Quinn |
| Ryan M. Williams | Amri Ackers |
| Jacob Proffitt | Robin Brande |
| Marian Goldeen | J.R. Murdock |
| Brenda Bergeron | Kathleen McClure |
| John Connelly | Michael Kelberer |
| Gary Speer | Gunnar Gunderson |
| Megan Bryce | F.I. Goldhaber |
| Michelle Tatam | Mary Jo Rabe |
| Ann Tucker | John Kilgallon |
| Kari Wolfe | Dave Hendrickson |

www.ingramcontent.com/pod-product-compliance
Lightning Source LLC
Chambersburg PA
CBHW081152170626
46813CB00009B/3169